Inka and Markus Brand with a story by Jens Baumeister

Translated by Britta Norris

EXIT THE BOOK

THE RYAN CREED CASE

A Puzzle Novel

PUZZLE WRIGHT PRESS
New York

PUZZLE
WRIGHT
PRESS
New York

Original title: Brand, Baumeister, *EXIT. Das Buch. Der Fall des Ryan Creed*

First published in 2024 in the United States and Canada by Puzzlewright Press, an imprint of Sterling Publishing Co., Inc. First published in Germany as *EXIT. Das Buch. Dwer Fall des Ryan Creed* in 2021 by Franckh-Kosmos Verlags-GmbH & Co. KG.

ISBN 978-1-4549-5869-7

For information about custom editions, special sales, and premium purchases, please contact specialsales@unionsquareandco.com.

Printed in Slovakia

Lot #:
10 9 8 7 6 5 4 3 2 1

08/24

unionsquareandco.com

English translation: Britta Norris
Authors: Inka and Markus Brand, Jens Baumeister
Illustrations: Thomas Moor
English-language puzzle consultant: Francis Heaney

WELCOME!

Do you love puzzles and enjoy reading exciting stories? Then EXIT: THE BOOK is perfect for you. It's packed with mysteries and exciting riddles. Ryan and Sarah are facing a dire situation; here's hoping you can help them!

Things you must do before you start:

First, cut out the three colored decoding strips (red, blue, and yellow) from pages 191 and 192, then insert them through the matching colored slots in the front cover flap. Also read page 190.

When you get to the end of a page, you will sometimes be asked to continue reading elsewhere in the book. Follow these instructions. Often you will come up against a riddle you must solve to crack a three-digit code. When you input the code in the decoder strips as directed, you'll get the page number on which to continue reading.

Everything you need to solve the puzzles is in this book! For some puzzles, you'll also need scissors, a pen, or some paper. Anything is possible; don't worry about cutting, labeling, creasing, folding, or tearing things in the book. But only cut things out that are surrounded by a dotted line, and only when the instructions tell you to do so.

If you get stuck, you will find clues and answers for each riddle on pages 184–187. Page 184 explains how to use the clues correctly. Only use them if you really need them. At the end of the story (page 188), count the number of clues you've used. The fewer clues you need, the better your final score will be.

Here's a quick recap:

1. Cut out the decoding strips on pages 191 and 192 and insert them into the matching colored slots in the front cover flap.
2. Start reading the story on page 005. Continue reading until you are told to go to a different page number, or there's a riddle to solve.
3. Solve the riddle. (Get ready to draw, cut, and fold). The solution is always a three-digit code, which you must enter into the decoding strips. Turn the strips over to get the page number on which to continue reading.
4. If you get stuck, use the clues and answers on pages 184-187 of the book to help you.
5. Work your way through the whole book, solving each riddle as you go, until you get to the end. Now start reading on page 005 and have fun!

005

The letter arrived near the end of class. Ryan had just checked his watch. He was right on schedule and had almost finished the planned material. Just as he was about to summarize the most important points, there was a knock on the door of the seminar room.

Ryan nodded to the students in his class. “One moment, please.”

Standing at the door was a courier in one of those well-designed corporate uniforms that suggested both fashionable nonchalance and affiliation with a large, reliable organization. He was in his late twenties – about Ryan’s age.

“Excuse me,” said the courier. “Could you ask Mr. Creed to come out? It’s a personal delivery.”

Ryan smiled. “You’re talking to him right now.” He pulled out his driver’s license to identify himself.

The courier blushed. “I’m sorry, Mr. Creed. I just thought.... You’re so young to be a lecturer.”

Ryan was used to this. In his first years of teaching, he’d often had students who were older than he was. He had never had to earn their respect – his reputation preceded him – but he was familiar with the surprised looks when they first met him.

“No problem,” Ryan replied, using his index finger to scribble an illegible signature on the device the courier held out to him. Then he accepted the delivery.

He assumed it was some kind of official correspondence. Not that he was expecting any – but who sent letters these days besides government agencies and advertising departments?

And besides, who would hire a courier service to deliver a letter that would interrupt him in the middle of class instead of using the regular mail service? But the letter must be personal – you could tell at first glance. It had been addressed in cursive and the postmark was stamped by hand, not with a machine. According to that postmark, it had been sent from the Seattle area.

"Have a nice day," the messenger said before disappearing down the corridor.

Ryan eyed the envelope skeptically, then tucked it into his jacket pocket and stepped back into the seminar room.

He sat down on the desk and resumed his presentation.

"Where were we? Oh, yes: in a way you can think of an encrypted text as a puzzle. There is exactly *one* correct solution, and usually exactly *one* possible way to get to it. And like other types of puzzles, encryption techniques fall into two broad categories. Do you know what they are?"

Immediately, several hands went up. Ryan surveyed the class for a moment before addressing one of the students.

It was always the same with freshmen: some were so eager to make a positive impression that their hands shot up at every question. Others were so afraid of looking stupid that they kept quiet even when they knew something. As a lecturer, Ryan felt it was his responsibility to strike a balance between these two groups.

So he ignored the raised hands and instead nodded to a young man in the second row. He hadn't said a word in class so far, but he had followed the lecture so closely that Ryan was pretty sure he would know the answer. "Could you tell us what two types of puzzles I'm talking about, Mr., uh...?"

"Anderson," the young man finished, and his voice didn't sound as shy as Ryan was used to from quiet freshmen. He pondered the question for a moment. "Hmm... well, there are puzzles where you know what to do, and others where figuring that out is itself part of the puzzle...?"

Although it was spoken more like a question than an answer, Ryan was satisfied because the student had gotten it correct.

"You're absolutely right, Mr. Anderson! The oldest encryption techniques were the equivalent of the matchstick puzzles I'm sure you've all seen: you spend hours thinking about the right approach to the solution, but once you've found it, the rest is a breeze. Modern encryption algorithms, on the other hand, are more like sudoku or crossword puzzles: the rules of the game are public knowledge, but the problem posed by the puzzle is so difficult that it takes a lot of work to find the solution."

Ryan saw a skeptical-looking student in the front row raise her hand. He had a hunch what her objection would be and beat her to it.

"This is, of course, a very, *very* gross oversimplification. So please don't go home thinking that the RSA algorithm works like a sudoku or a crossword puzzle."

He saw the hand being lowered again. Ryan had to smile. People were often easier to figure out than a well-designed puzzle. “Still,” he added, “you can learn something from both types of classic puzzles. That’s why you’ll find some of them on the server, for your homework. You have until Sunday to email me your results – including an explanation of your approach. Good luck, and see you next week!”

Ryan stood up and opened the seminar room door, signaling to everyone that the lecture was over.

When he returned to his desk, a number of students were already waiting for him. They had precisely the questions Ryan was expecting: organizational minutiae about server access, absences, grading criteria, and the like. Ryan patiently explained everything.

Within a few minutes, he had answered all of their questions. Only one person was still waiting: the young man to whom he had addressed his last question.

“Mr. Anderson? How can I help you?”

Confidently, the student looked him in the eye. “Mr. Creed, I don’t mean to offend you, but I think I and many others in this class were hoping for more than you’ve delivered so far.”

Ryan raised his eyebrows. “More? In what way?”

“Well, more practical application. I mean modern-day uses. Roman ciphers and riddles are well and good, but given your background, I’m sure you have insight into much more groundbreaking techniques. Don’t you?”

Ryan sighed. He was familiar with these objections. He could even understand them. After all, it was common knowledge that he had, conservatively speaking, a certain amount of practical experience in modern cryptography.

He could understand that people would enroll in his course to benefit from it. After all, his past was one of the reasons he had gotten this job in the first place. What they couldn't know was that Ryan had long since decided that it would be better for his talent to remain completely untapped in the future.

He looked at the student and shook his head. "Mr. Anderson, the course catalog outlines the content of my course quite precisely: 'An Introduction to the Theory of Cryptography Using Empirical Examples.' And that's exactly what I'm going to deliver. If you are not satisfied, you are, of course, free to transfer."

Anderson blushed slightly and lowered his eyes. Ryan knew this kind of reaction: someone had gone a little too far and was beginning to feel intimidated by their own courage.

"No, I have no desire to do that," the student clarified. "But I thought... you have so much relevant experience. Why don't you teach a class on that?"

"I have my reasons," Ryan explained curtly. "Besides, my knowledge in this area is not as up to date as you might think. In fact, it's about as current as it was a few years ago. And I'm doing my best not to brush up on it."

The student looked at Ryan for a moment, puzzled, then shrugged. "All right, well, thanks. See you next week, then."

When Anderson had left, Ryan put the rest of his papers into his bag. As he did, he remembered the letter in his jacket pocket and pulled it out. It was thin. Probably just one sheet, two at the most.

He ruled out that it could be private mail. He didn't know anyone in the Seattle area. So, probably advertising. Ryan regularly placed high in national puzzle contests, and some companies wanted to capitalize on that. They sent him promotional messages framed in puzzles, hoping Ryan would post about them on social media and spread their ads for aftershave, energy drinks, and computer games around the world.

Ryan thought this was a pretty sure sign that the marketing departments of these companies hadn't even bothered to take a minute to find out more about him. If they had, they would have quickly discovered that Ryan's accounts on the major social media platforms were all empty and set to private.

His previous job had taught him enough about the implications of data collection to avoid it as much as possible.

It was unusual, however, for such an ad to be sent by courier. Someone obviously had a very large budget. If a large enough chunk of it had gone into puzzle development, the letter might at least pose some challenge.

Curious, he tore open the envelope.

He immediately realized that his hunch was correct. It was indeed a riddle, since the letter didn't contain a single word, just a sequence of strange symbols.

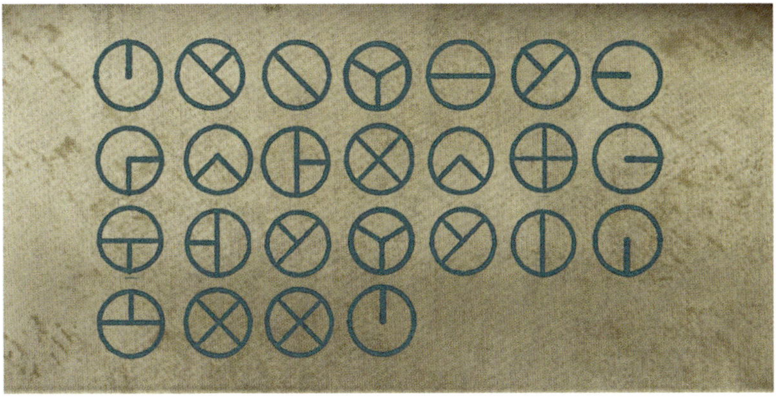

He examined the envelope and the letter from every angle, but there was nothing unusual about it. And no return address. For a moment, he toyed with the idea of starting to work on the solution right away, but then he decided against it. He still had to prepare for tomorrow's lesson. And as much as he liked puzzles, he already knew what the result would be: a ridiculous slogan for some product he didn't need. What else could it be? He slipped the page and envelope into his briefcase and left the seminar room.

On his way out, he checked his phone, an ancient device with a keypad and an LCD display. There was a missed call, with a voicemail. Ryan knew the number well: it was the office phone of Jamie Cook, a lawyer friend of his.

"Ryan, it's Jamie. I thought we agreed that you wouldn't send me any more clients until there was money in the Foundation account. I have no idea how it works for you, *but I actually need to* make money *from my work from time to time. Please call me back, OK?"*

Ryan sighed. The Foundation. It was a project he had started after leaving the police force, in response to his experiences while on active duty. The basic idea of the Foundation was to help victims of the justice system – people who had been wronged by the police, whether through excessive force, fabricated evidence, or improper interrogation methods. In short, abuse of power by officers.

Whenever he was asked why he felt so strongly about this issue, Ryan always gave the same answer. The same one he had just given to Mr. Anderson: "I have my reasons."

Ryan had invested all of his savings in the Foundation, all of the prize money from puzzle contests went into it, and he constantly solicited donations. Still, the Foundation was perpetually short of money, even though Jamie was taking on its cases at a friendship rate. In Ryan's eyes, it was evidence that more and more people were suffering as a result of the arbitrary actions of the security agencies.

In Jamie's eyes, it was a sign that Ryan couldn't say "no" or manage finances.

And Ryan had to admit, she was probably not entirely wrong.

He put the phone away. Of course he would call her back, he told himself.

But not until he had something to answer her with. Well, something other than "You're right, we don't have enough money."

Ryan thought about the riddle letter again. Maybe it wasn't an advertisement, but a competition? Those were rare, but they did take place. Competitions were usually held in public, though, not sent to unsuspecting participants in unsolicited envelopes with no return address. No, Ryan decided, everything still pointed to advertising.

Continue reading on page 072.

014

"Don't bother, Hector!" Ryan shouted at the hulking bodyguard who was trying to clear the collapse site. "We won't be getting out that way."

"He's right," Smith spoke up now. "You better see what it looks like on the other side."

Smith pointed to the dark tunnel leading out of the cave on the opposite side that no one in the group had explored yet.

Hector did as instructed. As he examined the passageways more closely, Smith kept the gun pointed at Ryan and Sarah.

There was a tense silence.

A few minutes later, Hector's voice rang out, and Ryan thought he could detect something like uncertainty in it: "Boss?"

"Yes?" Smith replied irritably.

"Boss, where are you?"

"Where I've been all along!"

"This place is a maze!"

It took Hector what seemed like an eternity to find his way back to them. And what he reported was less than encouraging: just beyond their current location, the tunnel branched off into countless passages, which themselves diverged again and again. It seemed impossible to determine which was the way out.

Smith cursed under his breath. "This is... very inconvenient." He looked at Ryan and Sarah. "Come on, we need something to mark the corridors with so we know which one is which! What do you have with you?"

015

Sarah was about to speak, but Ryan beat her to it. "I don't think that's necessary. We know something you don't. Specifically, how to get out of here!"

Smith raised his eyebrows. "What do you mean?"

"Reginald Dash *planned* this cave-in. The cage around the box was constructed in such a way that it couldn't be avoided. And with the box was a puzzle that could show us the way out." Ryan gestured to the collapse behind him. "Unfortunately, that puzzle is now buried under several tons of earth. But lucky for you, *I've* memorized it."

Smith smiled. "I see. So you want to offer me a deal: I want to get out of here, you know how. But why should I take you up on it? I'm armed. If I want your help, I can make sure I get it – with or without your deal."

"That's not really a threat as long as we're stuck here," Ryan replied. "In fact, death by firing squad would probably be less agonizing than slowly dying of thirst underground. Which, by the way, is considered one of the most torturous deaths of all – because the body knows exactly what it's lacking, and the victim becomes increasingly panic-stricken as they struggle to find water somewhere."

Unfazed, Smith shook his head. "So, you would really be willing to sacrifice your own life to prevent me from getting out of here, Mr. Creed? And not just your own. Your colleague's as well."

"Spare us the mind games!" Sarah interrupted him. "You threatened my daughter. And you know *very* well that I'm prepared to do anything for her."

Ryan glanced at Hector to see how the bodyguard was reacting to the prospect of his imminent death. If it unsettled the gruff man in any way, he hid it masterfully, still pointing the gun directly at Ryan and Sarah. Smith, however, paced around pensively for a few seconds, then approached Ryan. "I respect a talented businessman. So let's get this deal done! You get us all out of here. What do you want in return?"

Ryan thought for a moment before answering. He now had Smith exactly where he wanted him. All he had to do was make sure he used this opportunity wisely.

"Two things," he finally said. "First, you promise me that nothing will happen to Sarah and her daughter."

"If that's all it takes, I'm happy to promise you that. Sarah has done her duty. There's no need for me to get my hands dirty."

Sarah breathed a sigh of relief.

Ryan nodded. "Good. Second, you and your colleague will dump your weapons. And if you still have people outside, you will instruct them to get rid of theirs as well."

Smith laughed in disbelief. "You can't be *serious,* Mr. Creed! You honestly expect me to throw away my biggest advantage?!"

"That's exactly right. You can tie us up for all I care, but as long as you and your people are threatening us with guns, I won't do anything to help you. Put your weapons away and I'm in."

Smith thought for a moment. Finally he said: "On one condition, Mr. Creed: your help will not be limited to finding the way out. You and Sarah will continue to assist me until I find the coins. After that, I will let you both go and never bother you again." He extended his right hand to Ryan. "Do we have a deal, Mr. Creed?"

Ryan thought it through. He didn't trust this "Mr. Smith." On the other hand, he suspected that the only way to solve the riddle Dash had set for them was with the help of the notebook. And that was now in Smith's hands. If Ryan had any hope at all of getting himself and Sarah out of here unscathed, he would have to work with this gangster.

Ryan took Smith's outstretched hand, desperately hoping that he was doing the right thing.

"I need Dash's notes," Ryan explained.

"I thought the riddle was on the metal plate," Smith inquired skeptically.

"It was. But there was also a warning against searching if you're *lacking knowledge*. That knowledge has to be in Dash's notes."

Smith hesitated for a moment, then handed the book to Ryan. "Don't you dare do anything stupid. If you intend to destroy these notes, Hector and I will have no problem inflicting great pain on both of you. Understand?"

Ryan swallowed hard and nodded.

Sarah looked at Smith with contempt. "He said he would work with you. And Ryan is a man of his word. I hope you are, too."

Ryan tried to block out the discussion and remember the verse.

Your next path lies beneath the sun.

This had sounded like nonsense to Ryan at first, but now he had some idea of its meaning.

He flipped through the notebook feverishly until he came across a drawing of a sun – and underneath it, something that might resemble a map.

This couldn't be a coincidence! But what did the other verses he had seen on the metal plate mean?

Once you arrive where you've been led,
The answer will be on your head.
The symbols may appear abstract,
But they're your code: complete, intact.

Ryan took a piece of coal and started drawing on the cave floor.

You don't have to use coal to draw on the floor, but a pair of scissors might come in handy. Then you can probably arrange the pieces into a map. But what do the verses from Dash's notebook have to do with this?

When Ryan entered the college building two days later, Travis approached him animatedly. “Ryan, what are you *doing* here? We agreed that you’d…”

“Don’t panic,” Ryan cut him off. “If you call the dean’s office, you’ll find that the donation has been credited in full and all the conditions about my absence have been removed. I’m allowed back in.”

The rotund man looked at Ryan in surprise. “Yes… but….” he stuttered. “Why doesn’t anybody tell me anything? It’ll throw the whole schedule off again!”

Ryan gave him a reassuring pat on the shoulder. “It’s no problem! I’ve already taken care of it.”

On his way to the seminar room, he saw that he had another voicemail. From Jamie. Damn, he had completely forgotten to call her back!

He quickly listened to the message.

“Ryan, I have no idea what is going on, but… where did all the money in the Foundation account come from? Are there any receipts for it? I mean, I’m happy, *don’t get me wrong, but can you imagine how the IRS is going to react when we present them with the bank statements? Please call me back, OK?”*

He couldn’t help but grin. Typical Jamie. When she saw a gift horse, the first thing she did was stare straight into its mouth, calculating how much she’d have to spend on food, board, and vaccinations.

He would call her back, of course. But not until after his first lesson.

022

“Good morning, everyone!” he greeted his class. “I hope you haven’t done anything to disgrace me in my absence.” He walked to the board and drew something on it.

“Do you know what this is?” he asked, but immediately answered his own question. “Of course you do; it’s Morse code. But this particular message is also a great example of how a well-known encryption method can be used in very unexpected ways.”

Go to page 188 to find out how you performed.

Sarah laughed. "*That's* the solution? That guy Dash was really cunning!"

Ryan nodded. "I would have liked to have met him. I think we would have gotten along well."

"When did you figure it out?" Sarah wanted to know.

"After I'd ruled out all the obvious options. A straight code would have been too primitive, and a simple pun on Dash's last name too easy."

Power clapped his hands. "I appreciate your banter, but it's getting late, and I'd like to get out of here before sundown. Do me the pleasure of opening the vault, Mr. Creed!"

The lock and hinges had taken a beating over the decades. Even with the right combination, Ryan needed a lot of strength to open the safe. For a moment, he thought his little feint with the rusty door might unexpectedly prove to be true. But then it finally moved. Slowly and haltingly, inch by inch, it revealed its contents to them.

Inside was a dark blue cloth pouch. Ryan's fingers trembled as he looked inside. Sure enough, it contained thirty gold coins. Thirty 1933 Double Eagles! Each coin was worth more than Ryan had made in his entire life.

It was a strange feeling to see so much wealth in such a small space, and the otherworldly glow of the gold made it all the more surreal.

Next to him, Sarah was also peering into the pouch, her eyes wide with amazement. "Wow, so *this* is what we risked our lives for."

Power cleared his throat. "If you're done gawking, I'd like to take what is mine now."

"What? Oh, of course." Ryan turned to hand the bag to Power, but the man raised his hand dismissively.

"That won't be necessary. Just put it back in the vault. My people will take care of it right there."

Meanwhile, two women from Power's squad had returned after escorting the prisoners away. One of them took the case Power was carrying, the other pulled out a small device with a gas canister that Ryan thought looked like a blowtorch.

"You might want to step back a bit," Power advised Ryan and Sarah. "Otherwise, things might get a little uncomfortable. The ladies are trained for this."

"What are you going to do?" Ryan wondered. "Are you dismantling the safe?"

Will shook his head. "Like I said, I'm only interested in its contents."

Ryan looked questioningly at Sarah, who just shrugged.

The two women opened the case and took out a black, oddly heavy-walled vessel into which they hung a metal insert. Then they took the coins from the bag and placed them inside.

Ryan looked at the burner and the bowl and suddenly understood what Power was about to do. This was some contraption to melt down the coins!

"You can't do that, Power!" shouted Ryan, agitated. "These coins are irreplaceable!"

"You said it yourself, Will: the material value is practically nothing compared to their collector's value!" Sarah agreed with Ryan. "Why would you want to destroy something like that? Did all this mean nothing to you? This is absurd!"

Power motioned for the two women on his team to stop what they were doing. Leaning over the pit, he took one of the coins from the vessel and held it in front of Ryan and Sarah.

"This is what you've been after all this time. Thirty gold pieces. I don't know how biblically sound you are, Creed, but I'm sure the parallel has crossed your mind, hasn't it?"

"Not so far," Ryan admitted, "but now that you've said it, I know what you mean. Thirty pieces of silver. The reward for betraying Christ."

"At least, if you believe the book of Matthew," Power confirmed. "Do you know how much that was worth back then?"

Ryan shook his head.

"Comparatively little," Power continued. "At best, four times an average monthly salary, maybe less. It doesn't even matter whether the event happened exactly like that or not. The important thing is that it sounded plausible to the audience of Matthew's Gospel. They heard it and thought to themselves, yes, that is conceivable. It's terrible that someone would betray the Son of God for that kind of money, but it doesn't sound completely implausible."

"I have no idea where you're going with this, Power," Ryan interjected.

"You know how much each of these coins is worth, Creed. And you've seen what that value has driven other people to do. Smith was willing to stop at nothing to get them. And believe me, he's not the only one. As long as these coins exist, there will be people who will bring suffering to the world because of them. Just to possess a handful of atoms arranged in a certain order at a certain time. If these coins had been minted at any other time no one would have given a damn about them."

Power casually tossed the multimillion-dollar coin back into the crucible and motioned for the two women to continue.

"I am destroying this arrangement, and what will remain is a simple precious metal alloy. Still valuable. But not a magnet for the greedy and gluttonous of this world. I'm doing humanity a favor."

"And that's something you can decide on your own, just like that, is it?" Ryan said in an accusatory tone. "*You* decide what's good for humanity?"

"I subscribe to the philosophy that everyone should improve the world to the best of their ability. And my abilities are a little more varied than what most are capable of."

There was a low hiss as the bluish flame erupted from the blowtorch.

One of the women held it right up to the coins in the metal basket, and Ryan and Sarah watched as the irreplaceable pieces slowly deformed like chocolate left out in the sun too long, dripping into the fireproof mold until not a single coin was left.

Not a single coin... Suddenly Ryan understood, the realization hitting him like a ton of bricks. He laughed. "You could have saved yourself all this talk about saving the world, Power. All you really care about is protecting your investment! Right?"

Power looked kindly at Ryan. "Go ahead, Mr. Creed."

"You told me that there is only one 1933 Double Eagle in private hands. But you never said who the owner of that coin was." Creed pointed directly at Power. "It's *you*, isn't it?"

Power smiled. "Guilty as charged."

Sarah's mouth fell open. "That means... you only cared about what *your* coin was worth! You didn't want its value to decrease if thirty more pieces suddenly appeared. Because it would no longer be unique."

Ryan nodded. "And all those noble explanations were a smokescreen to distract from that."

Power was unimpressed. "Do you really think so, Mr. Creed? Could it not be possible that I have done a service to humanity as *well* as myself?"

Ryan snorted contemptuously. "I don't think you're really capable of a selfless act, Power. You disgust me."

Will Power pulled out his checkbook. “I am very sorry to hear that. Nevertheless, I would like to settle my debt. We had already agreed on an amount.”

Power scribbled and held the check out to Ryan.

For a moment, Ryan considered whether he really wanted to accept money from this man.

Power seemed to know what Ryan was thinking. “I don’t expect you to like me, Mr. Creed, and I don’t expect you to agree with everything I do. But I *do* believe that there are issues where our interests overlap. And I also believe that I can count on your support when the time comes.”

“Can’t say I agree with you, *sir,*” Ryan replied. But he accepted the check.

Power turned to Sarah. “By the way, Sarah? I’ve since learned about your deal with Mr. Smith.”

Sarah held his gaze. “I had no choice, Will. He threatened my daughter.”

Will shook his head. “Of *course* you had a choice! You could have let me in on it. And I fully expect you to do so next time. I know people who are excellent at taking care of such things.”

Sarah looked at Power in surprise. “That means... I’m not fired?”

“If I fired all the people who cared more about their family than their job, I’d end up surrounded by self-centered idiots. And that wouldn’t be good for business.”

Power turned and started walking toward the pit with the safe, then stopped and turned around once more.

029

ALY

“Oh, by the way, Sarah. Take the day off. Go to the beach. You and your daughter deserve it.”

Sarah sighed. “You *do* realize this is a terribly patriarchal, condescending gesture, don’t you, Will? Patronizingly treating the female employee to a few days at the beach with the kid.”

“Well, if you *prefer*, you’re welcome to continue working without any downtime at all.”

Sarah grinned. “No, thanks. Sometimes it’s worth making a deal with the patriarchy so you can beat them at their own game.”

As Power climbed down into the pit to join the two women, Ryan looked at Sarah in surprise. “You have more hidden depths than I realized when we first met.”

Sarah smiled. “There are a *lot* of sides to me you haven’t seen yet.” She hesitated and looked down for a moment before continuing. “If you want, we could change that.”

Ryan also eyed the floor. “I... I don’t think it’s right for me. This? This isn’t my world.”

“But you handled yourself well.”

“Yes, but I don’t really *want* to ‘handle myself well’ in shit like *this*. I’ve got something going at the college. Something I can use to help people who really deserve it.” He glanced sideways at Will Power. “And not the ones who can afford it. It wouldn’t be for you. Too boring. Just like your life is too exciting for me.”

Thoughtfully, Sarah ran her fingers through her hair.

"Your college looked kind of nice. Are you sure they don't need a helicopter pilot there?"

"Not too often. And the locks don't have to be picked regularly. And if they do, the janitor takes care of it."

Sarah had to smile. "But karate. *Surely* you have a need for a karate instructor?"

Ryan couldn't help but grin, too. "Oh, *sure.* Sure. Karate and cryptography are practically two sides of the same coin."

They were silent for a moment. Then Sarah looked at him seriously. "I still think you're right. College life and the Midwest wouldn't be for me. Much too safe. Too bad."

Ryan nodded. "Yeah, too bad. Maybe I'll come visit you sometime."

He didn't really believe it himself when he said it. But it felt right to say it in that moment. Because the desire was real: he would love to come back. But he knew he wouldn't.

Sarah seemed to have the same thought. "You know, your hotel is booked for a few more days."

"Thanks, but I think it's best if I get back as soon as possible." He tugged at the lumberjack shirt. "At least as soon as I get rid of this spy shirt."

"Your stuff is still at the motel. I'll fly you over if you want. And from there straight to the airport."

Ryan was taken aback. "You want to land at the motel in a *helicopter*?"

Sarah grinned. “Why not? There was no sign anywhere in the parking lot that said it wasn’t allowed.”

He laughed. “All right, then! I’ll have something to talk about when I get home.”

With that, he followed Sarah to the helicopter Smith had used to bring them here.

Continue reading on page 021.

0 3 2

Smith was brandishing his gun. "Come on, Creed, move it! Open the safe!"

Slowly, Ryan turned the wheel of the lock. Would this combination open the vault? If it did, what would happen to him and Sarah? And if it didn't, would Smith have the patience for another attempt?

There was only one way to find out. Ryan set the last digit and rattled the safe door. It was still firmly locked!

Smith was losing patience. "You're playing with your life, Creed! If you can't open this safe, you're a dead man!"

That was a creative approach! Keep it in mind for later because you're already on the right track. But you're not there yet.
Take another close look at Dash's riddle on page 125.

033

Ryan and Sarah stared in disbelief at Smith, who was rolling on the ground and holding his bleeding leg.

Then they noticed movement in the distance. A gunman in camouflage was running toward them, followed by three other men and women in combat gear.

All of them were clearly in good physical shape – they covered the distance in seconds and didn't even seem to be out of breath afterwards.

The squad operated without a word, like a well-rehearsed team. Three of them each took one of the gangsters and tied him up, and the last one pulled out a knife and cut Sarah's bonds.

Ryan began to suspect what was going on, and a moment later his suspicions were confirmed. A tall, bald man with a small briefcase in hand stepped out of the woods, looking quite relaxed: Will Power!

"I'm sorry I couldn't get here sooner. My people had to park the chopper far enough away that it wouldn't be heard."

Ryan climbed out of the pit and pointed to the combatants. "You have a private army?"

"Not exactly, but I'm a man who knows where to get what one might need."

"And how did you find us here?" Ryan wondered.

Power smiled. "That's an irony you especially will enjoy." Power patted Ryan's shoulder. "You made sure of it yourself all along."

It took Ryan a moment to realize what he meant. "The clothes...?"

Power nodded. “Normally I would have installed a tracking program on your phone. But one, someone with your expertise might have noticed, and two, your phone is simply too antique for that, if you’ll pardon the expression. That’s why I had these custom-made for you.”

Power pointed to the sleeves of the shirt. “There are high performance antennas in the seams, GPS receivers in the shoulders, and a transmitter with enough battery power for three days in the hem. It’s fascinating how tiny electronics can be these days if you can afford them, don’t you think?”

Ryan was speechless. He turned to Sarah. “Did you know about this?”

Sarah shook her head. “No, but I should have guessed.”

Ryan watched as the squad led Smith and his cronies away.

“He said you and he had history?” he asked Power.

The man nodded. “I think I trampled a few of his sandcastles with my activities. Not that I’m sorry. For one thing, my business is more profitable than his, and for another, it has the advantage of being legal.”

“I was thinking something along those lines,” Ryan replied. “And what will happen to him and his people?”

“I have good connections with the local authorities. There are some people who have been after this cohort for a long time, and when it comes down to it, they don’t really care how they get them.”

Ryan shook his head. "I suppose you think you can buy *anything,* don't you?"

"I don't *think* I can, Mr. Creed. I *know* I can. Just like I know that vault door isn't really rusted in. What you gave Smith wasn't the right solution, was it?"

Ryan sighed. That creep was right. "Correct. The vault door isn't stuck. It's still locked."

Sarah looked at him in astonishment. "But you explained the approach to him!"

"The approach was nonsense. And the Morse code was wrong!" Ryan explained. He climbed into the pit, pulled the sleeve of his shirt... his *damn spy transmitter shirt...* down over his wrist a bit and wiped it over the characters on the vault – and they suddenly changed!

"I still had the piece of coal from the mine with me," Ryan continued. "And I needed time to stall these guys. So I made sure the puzzle was impossible to solve." He smiled slightly. "*Now,* on the other hand, it *should* be solvable."

Sarah hesitated as she deciphered the Morse code. "OK, that's just gibberish, right?"

Ryan nodded. "True, but I noticed that by adding some markings, it would be relatively easy to make words out of the gibberish that would throw Smith off the scent. But the real clue is hidden somewhere else. Can you figure it out?" He looked at Sarah expectantly.

Sarah might be able to figure it out if she turned it over in her mind long enough. What about you? Can you find the solution? It is still connected to the name itself.

---

0 3 7
YAL

Ryan explained the concept of the puzzle to Sarah. “All these piles of coal and stacks of wood must have been left here by Reginald Dash himself. It must have taken a lot of work.”

“He did it for his son,” Sarah murmured.

“How do you mean?”

“Well, he wanted to leave the coins to his son, Stuart. No doubt he was happy to go to all this trouble just for that.”

They turned into the corridor Ryan had identified as the correct one.

“Do you think Stuart was still alive when Reginald set up this stash?” Ryan wondered. “It must have taken a while to get everything ready. Maybe Stuart was dead by then.”

“No!” Sarah replied unexpectedly vehemently. “If his son were dead, Reginald Dash wouldn’t have gone through with this. He wouldn’t have given a damn.”

Ryan looked at her in surprise. Sarah’s face had taken on a grim expression and she seemed to be staring off into the distance instead of concentrating on the route.

He stopped walking. “Hang on, now you’re the one who’s day-dreaming. What’s going on?”

Sarah said nothing but motioned for him to continue following her. Ryan stood his ground. “Come on, Sarah. Why won’t you talk to me?”

Sarah repeated her silent gesture. She looked directly at Ryan and he noticed that she had tears in her eyes.

He had no idea what this was all about, but he realized that he shouldn't push Sarah any further. He followed her deeper into the mine.

They walked side by side in silence for a few minutes before they came to a rusty mine cart that had gone off the rails in front of a tunnel entrance.

According to the map, this was the tunnel they had to go through.

Without saying a word, they heaved the wagon out of the way and then bent down to squeeze through the tunnel, one after the other.

Sarah was still silent, having dried her tears by that point. Ryan let her be. He was confident that she would eventually tell him what was going on.

When they came out on the other side of the tunnel, Sarah paused and pulled out her cell phone.

"Zero reception," she muttered. "Good, then I guess we're deep enough."

Sarah tapped on her phone for a moment and showed Ryan a photo of a girl. The same narrow face as Sarah's, the same dark hair. "This is Cathy," she said quietly. "My daughter."

Ryan nodded, but he didn't understand what she was getting at.

"I'm like Reginald Dash," Sarah continued. "I'm doing this because of her. *Only* because of her."

"What do you mean?" Ryan asked cautiously. "Working for Power?"

"No, not that. But..." Sarah's voice broke. She took a moment to collect herself, then continued: "The guys in the SUV – they threatened me. That they would hurt Cathy."

"What? When?"

"A few weeks ago. Somehow, they must have realized that Will had found the book. They didn't dare approach him directly... but they *did* approach *me*." Sarah stared at the floor. "They showed me pictures of Cathy. Taken really close up. And said they could come for Cathy at any time."

"Holy shit, Sarah. Did you tell the police about this? Or Will?"

Sarah shook her head. "They said if anyone found out, I'd never see Cathy again. I couldn't take that chance." Sarah unzipped her vest and shined her flashlight on a dark sphere near her collar. "That's a microphone. With a transmitter. They can listen in on me any time they want. Except down here – at least, I *hope* they can't."

Ryan stared at Sarah. "That's how those guys knew where we were? Because they were listening the whole time?"

"I tried to keep them from following me so closely. When you weren't in the room, I tried talking into the microphone to explain that they could trust me and didn't have to watch me all the time – but it made no difference."

Ryan exhaled sharply. "Do you know anything about these guys?"

"Their leader calls himself Smith. That's probably not his real name."

Ryan laughed. "Will Power and Mr. Smith – why do people always take such ridiculous aliases?" He looked at Sarah. "And what was your plan? Why didn't you just give them the notebook?"

"They heard you were coming and wanted you to do the work."

"I see – I find the coins, then *these* guys swoop in and pocket them. Something like that?"

Sarah nodded regretfully. "I really wanted to keep you out of it. That's why I didn't want you to come down here with me."

"You were going to run off with the coins and take them to Smith."

"Then it would be over and you couldn't be blamed," she said.

Ryan was silent for a moment. "Where is Cathy now?"

"With my mother. It was arranged some time ago. Mom doesn't know anything. As long as I follow the rules, nothing will happen to either of them."

"What about Cathy's father? Where is he?"

She sighed. "I'd like to know that, too. Let me know if you find that asshole anywhere."

Ryan leaned against one of the tunnel walls and tried to process what he had heard. "There's one thing I don't understand," he finally said. "From what I can see, you're pretty tough. Tougher than most men I know. And..."

"Stop it!" Sarah interrupted him firmly. "Please don't turn this into some misogynist bullcrap, OK? This isn't about me as a woman – it's about me as a *parent*. Any father or mother in my position would have done the same thing. And I'm not sorry for what I did. I'm just sorry I dragged you into it."

It would have been easy for Ryan to judge her. Sarah might've thought she had no other way out, but Ryan wasn't so sure. She had an employer with virtually unlimited wealth, many extraordinary talents of her own, and obviously a great deal of experience in navigating legal gray areas.

Wasn't she too smart to be manipulated into such a position?

Perhaps. But Ryan himself knew only too well that intelligence and experience didn't always protect you from making stupid, momentous mistakes...

"Creed! What's new in the exciting world of cybercrime?" Marcus had entered Ryan's office without knocking. As always.

"I beat my best time at sudoku by five seconds," Ryan replied dryly.

"Uncle Sam really does pay you too much money."

"I've been saying that for years. And yet you hired me."

The deal with the FBI had turned out to be a stroke of luck for Ryan. Not only had the charges against him been dropped, but he had been offered a lucrative consulting contract – and a full-time job right out of high school.

Of course there were days that were dull. Like today, for example. Watching a computer decrypt a hard drive for hours on end was anything but entertaining.

All in all, though, Ryan had found his dream job. Every day brought new challenges and puzzles, and whenever he managed to solve a particularly tricky problem, he felt that he had helped to serve justice.

But the best part of the job was his colleagues. Especially Marcus. From the outset, the agent had looked out for Ryan. In front of his parents, he had praised Ryan's computer skills so enthusiastically that they had ended up almost proud of their boy, despite the fact that he had just been busted by the FBI. And Marcus had also made sure that Ryan quickly learned the ropes of government life. He had opened doors, rolled out red carpets, the works.

It was not that he had any favoritism for Ryan. No, it was just the way Marcus treated everyone in the department, bar none. He was the guy who invited people over for barbecues in the summer, the guy who sent out e-mails to collect contributions for people's birthday presents, and the guy who was always the first to donate when someone raised money for a good cause.

He was also a damn good agent.

No doubt about it: Marcus was one of the good guys. Ryan had realized that from the first time he sat down with him at the kitchen table, and it had proven true again and again after that.

"I need your help. Cell phone surveillance on a dealer. With a motion log, if possible," Marcus had explained to him that day.

Ryan sat up at his desk and picked up a legal pad. "Smartphone or flip phone?"

"Smartphone. Not sure what operating system."

"Doesn't matter. I can find out. You have the number, right?"

"Sure." Marcus handed him a slip of paper.

"OK. As soon as you get the court order, I'll get on it."

Marcus hesitated for a moment, then closed the office door. "I don't have it here right now."

"What do you mean, 'don't have it here'?"

Marcus looked down awkwardly. "I was late. We just found out at the last minute that a deal was going ahead. I filled out the paperwork, but they're taking their time in court."

Ryan knew the problem. The judiciary didn't always have the same sense of urgency as the investigating authorities. "You know you can't use any of this in court if you don't have a warrant?" Ryan asked.

"I've been doing this job a few decades longer than you. And you know me. Of course I'm careful. I just want to be ready when the warrant comes in and we're allowed to use the data. Anything we collect before then will be destroyed unseen. And if we don't get the warrant, you'll undo the hack. Agreed?"

Ryan sighed. It wasn't completely clean. If the defense got wind of this in a trial, the entire presentation of evidence would be open to challenge.

"This is really urgent," Marcus interrupted his thoughts. "We've been working on this for over a year. We're damn sure we know what's going on, but we don't have enough evidence to arrest them yet. And if we don't act now, these guys will probably be in South America the day after tomorrow, and we'll never see them again. So we have nothing to lose."

Ryan looked at the phone number Marcus had written down for him. "OK. I'll do it. But make sure you catch the guys, OK?"

"Of course. It's a matter of honor!"

Ryan had later testified before the internal investigation committee that Marcus's arguments had convinced him. It was even true, and that was embarrassing enough. Because with a little distance, he had quickly realized how thin and predictable the excuses were, and how easy it would have been to dismiss them.

But this wasn't what Ryan was most ashamed of. What really bothered him, and what he hadn't told the committee at the time, was that he had done it because he was bored. The prospect of a few more hours of mindless computer babysitting had seemed so tedious that Ryan had thrown caution to the wind and accepted Marcus's assignment.

It was surprisingly easy to install software on other people's devices. Of course, the simplest way was to get the target to download the program by disguising it as something benign. A game, for example, or an application with some kind of utility value.

But that wasn't slick enough for Ryan. It depended on the victim playing along. They had to get the app from somewhere and not get suspicious at some point and take a closer look at it or even delete it.

It was much better if they didn't even notice what was happening on their phone.

045

And fortunately, Ryan knew of plenty of security loopholes that made this possible: a silent text message here, a tailored data package there. If you asked an internet-connected device the right questions, it would eventually give you the exact answer you needed to gain access.

No different than a puzzle, Ryan thought. Just one with a little more at stake than the usual contests. The prize for him: a warm feeling. The prize for the person under surveillance: a court date and at least a few years in jail.

In this case, it hadn't taken him long to find the right sequence of commands. In less than an hour, Ryan had installed an invisible program on the phone that would periodically transmit the phone's exact location to Marcus's computer.

Two days later, the owner of the phone was dead. Shot to death. Lying beside her was Marcus's body, a gun in his hand.

The victim and Marcus had been in a relationship years before, but it had ended. She had moved on. Marcus hadn't. She had complained to the police several times that he was stalking her, but no one had taken her seriously. After all, Marcus was an FBI agent – and one of the good ones. No doubt it was all hysteria. She shouldn't make such a fuss.

She had been shot at close range. With Marcus's service weapon. He had ambushed her in a park where she jogged regularly.

She had always had her cell phone with her when she went jogging. For safety reasons.

An internal investigation had cleared Ryan of any wrongdoing.

046

Sure, installing the app was against regulations – but he was only following the orders of a superior officer. He couldn't have expected Marcus to abuse his position like this. The whole thing had been an unfortunate isolated incident, and the person solely responsible had already brought himself to justice.

Ryan's boss had offered him a leave of absence. Ryan had sent her his letter of resignation.

That was the guilt he had carried with him ever since, no matter where he went. That was the mistake he had made and the consequences that followed.

What right did he have to judge Sarah? Even intelligent people sometimes made stupid decisions. And Sarah's reasons were a million times better than his. She was trying to protect her daughter. He had simply been bored, and hacking a cell phone had seemed more exciting than twiddling his thumbs and waiting for the computer to do its job.

Continue reading on page 116.

047

When Ryan woke up the next morning, Sarah was already dressed. She sat at the narrow desk, sipping from a paper cup and scrolling on her smartphone.

"Morning! Coffee machine's downstairs." She grimaced. "Though if I were you, I'd get one on the road. This stuff is *undrinkable*."

Ryan thanked her for the warning.

"What are you up to?" he asked. "Trying to find out about our pursuers yesterday?"

"What? *Them?* Nah!" Sarah's tone was contemptuous. "I wouldn't worry about them. They're amateurs."

"How can you be so sure?"

"Because I have years of experience with this sort of thing," she said with a knowing look.

"Experience with being followed by strangers?" Ryan asked.

"Experience in assessing danger. And those guys yesterday were a nuisance, but not much of a threat. That's why they were so easy to shake off."

She held up her phone. "Just researching what our find from yesterday might be about."

"You uncover anything yet?"

"I won't tell you until you put some clothes on. As a matter of principle, I don't have business conversations with men wearing just a T-shirt and underpants."

"Did you learn *that* from experience, too?"

"No. I learned it from my banker. He shares the sentiment."

Ryan laughed and disappeared into the bathroom with the shopping bags to get dressed.

The clothes Sarah had bought fit him perfectly. But Ryan was only mildly surprised: apparently, his body was fairly consistent with the manufacturers' standard measurements, and he rarely had trouble finding clothes that fit.

From a fashion point of view, they weren't exactly his cup of tea: they had a little too much of an outdoor adventure look. On the other hand, it probably suited the environment. As Sarah had said, the wilderness was always just a few minutes' drive away.

A minute later, he emerged from the bathroom and Sarah nodded approvingly. "*There* you go! We're going to turn you into a real trapper."

"Right now I feel more like I've stepped out of a lumberjack equipment catalog."

"Doesn't everyone in the Midwest walk around in cowboy gear all day? Here, it's all about the lumberjack look."

Ryan grinned. "I just moved to the area, and I haven't had time to buy a ten-gallon hat. And besides, I'm a college lecturer. So it's quasi-compulsory for me to walk around in threadbare tweed jackets and corduroy pants."

She laughed. "Don't worry, as long as you use words like 'quasi,' everyone will know you're a nerd under it all."

Sarah had placed the strange coin from the night before on the table in front of her. Now, in broad daylight, he would be able to examine it more closely.

"Were you able to figure anything out?" he asked.

Sarah nodded. "A little. But I need more." She handed Ryan her phone. It showed an email she had just received from the U.S. Mint.

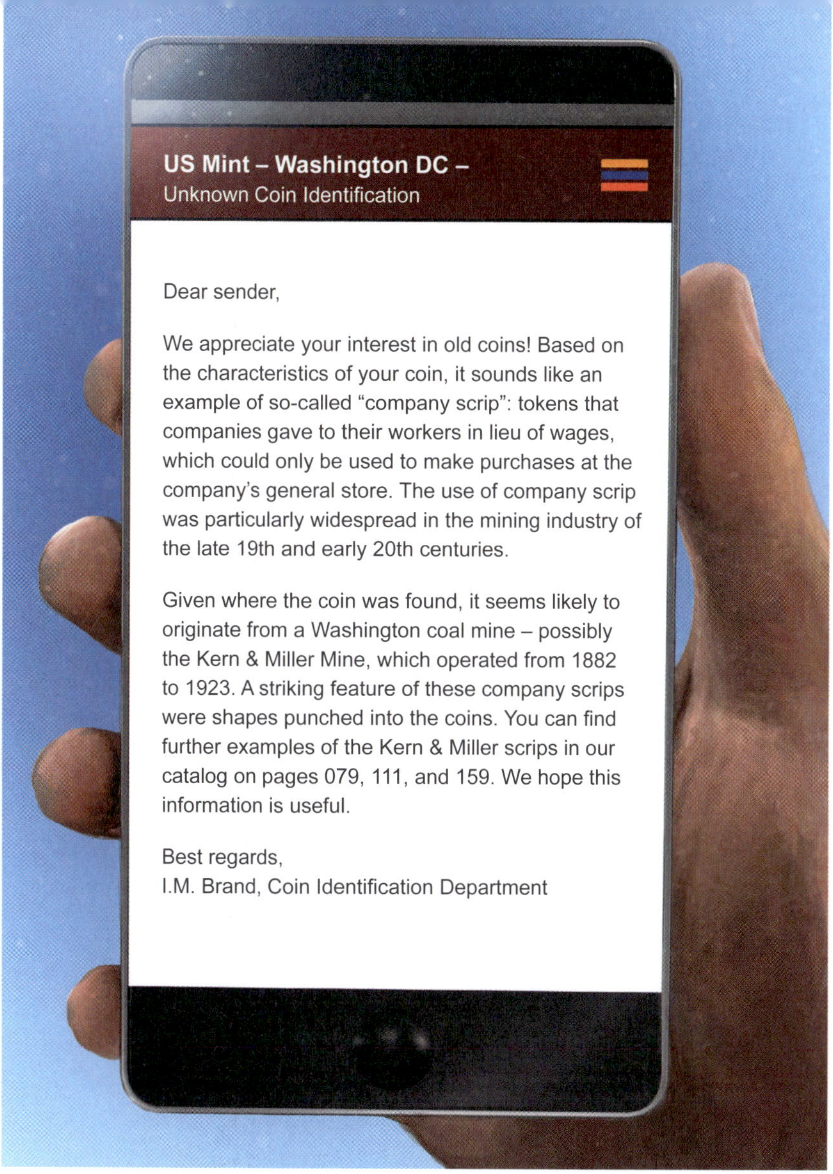

US Mint – Washington DC –
Unknown Coin Identification

Dear sender,

We appreciate your interest in old coins! Based on the characteristics of your coin, it sounds like an example of so-called "company scrip": tokens that companies gave to their workers in lieu of wages, which could only be used to make purchases at the company's general store. The use of company scrip was particularly widespread in the mining industry of the late 19th and early 20th centuries.

Given where the coin was found, it seems likely to originate from a Washington coal mine – possibly the Kern & Miller Mine, which operated from 1882 to 1923. A striking feature of these company scrips were shapes punched into the coins. You can find further examples of the Kern & Miller scrips in our catalog on pages 079, 111, and 159. We hope this information is useful.

Best regards,
I.M. Brand, Coin Identification Department

Do some additional research about the coin to unlock the code for the number of the page to read next.

050

They stepped through the door and found themselves in a long cobblestone alley. It smelled musty and the skylights let in a little light that Ryan guessed must be from the streetlamps. The skylights had to be the glass bricks they had seen on the sidewalk earlier.

The dim light was enough for them to get their bearings. The path was secured by railings on either side, behind which the museum staff had decoratively arranged junk from the past hundred years. Old billboards, gears, water heaters, car parts, and unidentifiable scrap metal served to remind visitors that they had entered a forgotten part of the city. Ryan wondered how much of this stuff actually came from down here and how much was just brought in for atmosphere.

One side of the alley was a continuous wall with wires and pipes running along it. The other side, however, was almost exactly what Ryan had seen in the small square above: narrow, old house facades with storefront entrances. Only here, they were below street level, and all of them looked as if they had been vacant for decades.

"How is it possible that this was just forgotten?" he wondered.

"The usual way," Sarah replied. "It was suppressed until no one remembered. After the passages were completely covered, fewer and fewer people came down here. And the more secluded they became, the more attractive they were to those who had good reasons for conducting business out of the public eye." Ryan nodded.

"Of course," Sara continued, "the residents weren't happy that criminals and the like were passing by their basement doors on a regular basis, so more and more people bricked up their doors and windows. Eventually, the city officially closed the remaining entrances and that was that. A generation or two later, no one even remembered what was under the pavement or behind the basement walls – until it was rediscovered by chance." She pointed to the right. "Madison Street should be that way."

Sarah deflected the flashlight's upward glow with her fingers to keep it from shining through the glass blocks onto the street. They passed more explanatory signs, squeezed under metal girders, rounded a corner – and came to a closed steel door.

"Looks like this is the end of the tour," Ryan said.

"The *public* tour," Sarah corrected him. "We booked the *behind-the-scenes package*. Hold this!" She handed Ryan the flashlight, pulled out her lockpicks, and started working on the lock. "Hmm, this one's a little harder than the one upstairs."

"Better quality?" Ryan wanted to know.

"On the contrary. Rusty. You can bet that no one has been through this door for ages. But I'm prepared for that, too." She pulled a can of rust remover from another of her vest pockets and sprayed some into the keyhole. Then she fiddled with the lockpick again. Seconds later, the lock clicked and the door opened.

Satisfied, Sarah smiled. "I should consider billing them, actually. For maintenance."

Behind the door, the atmosphere of the passage changed – instead of the staged ghost train feeling of the exhibition areas, Ryan felt a real sense of unease. Instead of decorative junk strewn about and vintage-style billboards leaning against the walls, there were cobwebs hanging from the ceiling and rats scurrying away from the beam of the flashlight. Only now did Ryan realize how much the old facades in the front section must have been restored, because the walls here looked dull, dirty, and unwelcoming by comparison.

"In any case, we needn't have worried about tourists discovering Reginald Dash's stash," Sarah remarked.

They moved forward cautiously, past withered mouse carcasses and dusty shards of glass. Sarah scanned the walls. Finally, she stopped at a door. Next to the entrance was a very faded house number: 635.

"That's it!" Sarah rattled the brittle door blocking the entrance. She hadn't shaken it too hard, but the wood still snapped at the top hinge. She gave it another hard shake and the whole door fell off its hinges.

Ryan raised his eyebrows in disapproval.

"What?" Sarah said. "That wasn't on purpose. It's not *my* fault that everything here is falling apart."

A musty smell wafted toward them as they entered the pitch-black room. Ryan coughed and covered his mouth and nose with his hand.

053

Sarah pulled out a dust mask from her pocket, put it on, and pointed the flashlight at the ceiling, bathing their surroundings in an even twilight. The room clearly had a tumultuous past. There was a half-rotted wooden bar in one corner, with a shelf behind it that held a few empty, dust-covered bottles. In front of it were the remains of old chairs and tables, obviously smashed to pieces by someone with a lot of energy. Vandalism, Ryan guessed. If a room sat empty for that long, someone would eventually come along and trash it.

He motioned to the bar. "This was a speakeasy, I take it?" Though he had often read about these hidden bars from the Prohibition era, he had never set foot in one. They had usually been set up in the backs of houses or in hidden basements – so, of course, an underground street was an ideal location.

Sarah nodded. "That's probably how Dash found out about this place."

Ryan looked around. The walls were covered in red fabric wall-paper with gold trim. Moths had destroyed much of the material, but the colors were still surprisingly vibrant. Probably because there was no sunlight down here.

Aside from the empty bar and the smashed furniture, there was nothing in the room that stood out.

"Whatever Dash was hiding here, I have no idea if it's still around," Ryan muttered.

"I'll see if I can find anything in the bar," Sarah said. "In the meantime, will you deal with the rest of the room?"

It was no easy task. Any movement stirred up dust, and insects had taken up residence in the crumbling furniture, fleeing in panic at the slightest disturbance. Nevertheless, Ryan tried to search everything for a message from Dash. Without success.

Finally, he shifted his attention away from the furniture and surveyed the rest of the room. The outlines of pictures that had once hung here were still visible on the walls, and there were bare metal rods that were probably the remains of sconces.

Something next to one of those rods caught Ryan's eye: the ornamentation looked a little different here than on the rest of the wallpaper. It almost seemed like... "Bring the flashlight over here!" he called to Sarah. "I think I got something."

She was beside him in an instant. Ryan showed her the spot, and when the beam of light hit the wall, there was no doubt: there on the wallpaper were two letters. "R" and "D." Reginald Dash's monogram, just like the one on the cover of the notebook!

Sarah ran her fingers across the wallpaper. "Feels normal, nothing here."

"Maybe on the back?" Ryan speculated. He stuck a finger into a rip in the wallpaper near the monogram and carefully tore it away from the wall. The back of the wallpaper was unremarkable – but the wall behind it certainly was not. It was mostly whitewashed, but where the light fixture's bracket protruded from the wall, there was a solid steel plate embedded in it – and the metal rod stuck out straight from its center.

Ryan tapped it. "Sounds pretty solid."

"A safe?" Sarah speculated.

Ryan took a closer look at the spot where the light fixture jutted out from the metal. It was engraved with small numbers, from zero to nine. "No doubt," he declared. "Is there anything in the notebook that looks like a combination?"

Sarah shook her head. "But maybe we'll find it here."

She pulled at a piece of wallpaper hanging down, revealing what had been painted on the wall behind: Dash's monogram again!

Sarah kicked gently at the spot on the wall with the monogram. It sounded hollow. "Take a step back," she instructed Ryan before grabbing a table leg that was lying on the floor and ramming it hard against the exposed wall. It cracked under the impact, the table leg leaving a hole the size of a fist. "It's very flimsy wood," Sarah explained. "Keep going!" She handed Ryan the table leg.

Again and again he banged the heavy piece of wood against the wall, surprised at how much he enjoyed clearing their path this way.

056

It felt good, liberating somehow, not to have to worry about the usual rules anymore, and Ryan suddenly remembered the first time he had felt like this....

Continue reading on page 159.

Ryan studied the Morse code for a while. "The text in it is just a distraction," he explained. "What's really important is Dash's name: we have to count the *dashes* in each line!"

Smith smiled. "Very well deduced, Creed. Open the safe!"

Ryan set the numbers and prepared himself for whatever was going to happen next. His and Sarah's fate was about to be decided.

As the last digit clicked into place, he pulled the handle. "It's moving!" he announced to Smith. "The code was right! But I can't get it to open all the way. Maybe the hinges are rusted?"

"Go on, Hector, take a look at it!" Smith ordered.

As the bodyguard climbed back into the pit, Ryan pushed himself to the side until he was within reach of Smith's feet. He watched as Hector began to fiddle with the safe door and saw Smith watching greedily, eager to finally get his hands on the coveted coins.

Now was the time!

"Sarah? *Go!*" Ryan yelled, stretching out his arms and pulling Smith's feet toward him. Smith lost his balance and dropped the gun as he tried to steady himself.

Out of the corner of his eye, Ryan saw Sarah whirl around and deliver a karate kick right under the chin of a stunned Gus. The pilot staggered backwards, then collapsed like a marionette whose strings had been cut.

Sarah lost her balance, but even with her hands tied, she rolled over her shoulder like a pro.

Hector, still fumbling with the safe, was caught off guard and turned on Ryan, who was standing right next to him in the pit. The bodyguard launched a punch that probably would have knocked Ryan out, but as he turned, Hector had inadvertently left himself open – open to the reach of Ryan's knee.

The burly bodyguard doubled over in pain as Ryan rammed his kneecap full force between the man's legs. Ryan grabbed the shovel leaning against the pit wall behind him and brought it down on Hector's head. The man let out a wheezing groan, then went down.

"Ryan, look out!" yelled Sarah, who was still tied up and lying on the ground close to Gus.

Instinctively, Ryan ducked, and a bullet from Smith's revolver whizzed past his head – Smith was back on his feet, gun in hand.

"You're *useless*, Creed! And it's time to get rid of you!" He pointed the gun directly at Ryan. There was no way he could miss.

Ryan closed his eyes and waited. "This is it," he thought. Seconds later, a shot echoed through the wilderness.

Continue reading on page 033.

Ryan had been alone when they arrived. Mom and Dad both worked, so there was usually no one around when he got home from school.

When the doorbell rang, Ryan thought it might be the mailman. But a quick glance out the window made him doubt that. Two men in dark suits. Ryan guessed one was around thirty, the other older. Maybe in his mid-forties, with glasses, a briefcase, a square lower jaw, and a short haircut.

Jehovah's Witnesses?

"I've already found God!" he called to them through the closed door. "No need."

The men rang the doorbell again.

"You're Ryan, right?" the shorthaired man asked through the door. "Ryan Creed. Or should I say 'E-RazOr'?"

Ryan was taken aback. How did this guy know his alias?

"I don't know what you're talking about!" Ryan shouted nervously.

Through the window, Ryan could see the man pull a printed sheet of paper out of his jacket pocket. But he couldn't see what was on it.

"Got something for you. From 'Doom98.'"

Was that possible? But why would Doom98 send people to his house? And how did he even know where Ryan lived?

There was a ping from Ryan's room. A message!

He hesitated. Should he go and check what it was? But then he'd have to leave those guys standing at his door. And he didn't know if that was a good idea.

Another ping. Someone was trying to tell him something urgent.

For a moment Ryan didn't know what to do, then he quickly fastened the security chain to the door. He didn't really expect these guys to kick the door down, but somehow the little chain made him feel safer.

"You don't have to be afraid of us," the shorthaired man assured him.

Ryan didn't even listen. He ran into his room and opened the messenger app.

== Doom98 has invited you to a private chat session. Will you accept? (Y/N)

And again below it:

== Doom98 has invited you to a private chat session. Will you accept? (Y/N)

Ryan pressed "Y".

== E-RazOr has joined the private chat.
== Doom98 has joined the private chat.
<E-RazOr> There are two guys at my door!
<E-RazOr> They say you sent them!
<E-RazOr> What should I do?
<Doom98> Relax. They're buddies of mine.
<Doom98> You can just let them in.
<E-RazOr> What do they want?
<Doom98> It's a surprise ;)
<E-RazOr> That's not an answer!
<E-RazOr> And how do they know my name and where I live?

<Doom98> I'm a hacker, remember?
<Doom98> Did you really think I didn't know who you were?
<E-RazOr> WTF???!!!
<Doom98> Relax, kid! Just relax!
<Doom98> Have I ever screwed you over?
<Doom98> I saved your ass on that log file thing.
<Doom98> So just trust me, OK?

He had a point: Doom98 had never caused him any problems. Quite the opposite, in fact. OK, the log file thing had happened over a year ago, and by now Ryan felt he was a better hacker than Doom98. But still, Ryan owed him. And if Doom98 said it was OK, then it probably was OK. Or was it?

<E-RazOr> All right. I'll let them in.
<Doom98> Good decision! Very good decision indeed!

Ryan made his way back to the front door where the two men were still waiting patiently. He unhooked the security chain and turned the knob to open the lock.

The door was only inches open when the younger man stuck his foot in the gap and used his shoulder to force it open. The older man pushed into the hallway and shoved the paper in Ryan's face.

"FBI!" he shouted. "Special Agent Steven Marcus. We have a search warrant."

062

More people in dark suits appeared from somewhere, running past Ryan into the house and dispersing into different rooms.

"What... what is this?" Ryan stammered.

"You have the right to remain silent," the man continued routinely. "Anything you say can be used against you in a court of law. You have the right to inform your parents before we question you. You have the right to consult with a lawyer before we question you. You have the right to have a lawyer present during questioning. If you or your parents cannot afford a lawyer, a public defender will be appointed at your request before questioning." He looked Ryan in the eye. "Any questions?"

Ryan was too stunned to answer right away.

"Found it!" one of the men shouted from Ryan's room, and immediately several of the others went running to him.

As if in a trance, Ryan followed behind, only to discover that they were tampering with his computer. One of them had inserted a USB flash drive and launched a program that now seemed to be copying data. Others were rifling through Ryan's closets and drawers, stuffing things into plastic bags and boxes.

They had even torn down the gaming poster on his door, probably to see if there was anything hidden behind it.

Ryan felt a hand on his shoulder. The shorthaired man had followed after him.

"Scary shit, isn't it?" he said, his voice sounding almost sympathetic.

Ryan nodded silently, paralyzed on the spot. He felt tears welling up inside him.

"It's OK," Agent Marcus said. "Come with me."

He led Ryan into the kitchen (His damn family's kitchen! What was an FBI agent doing here?!) *and poured him a glass of water.*

"Shall we sit down?" He gestured to the chairs at the kitchen table. They were tacky, clunky wooden things with thick cushions that Mom had picked up cheap at a garage sale years ago.

"I thought you weren't allowed to question me without my parents present," Ryan said carefully.

"I don't intend to question you," Agent Marcus replied calmly. "I just want to tell you something. You can keep your mouth shut, for all I care. But I thought you might be curious as to why we showed up here in the first place, right?"

Of course Ryan was curious. But he was also wondering why this guy wanted to tell him anything. The cops on TV never told suspects anything.

"How do I know you're not bullshitting me?"

"Because I have no reason to. Everything I'm about to tell you is one hundred percent verifiable. Whether you know about it or not makes no difference to us, but it might make a difference to you. And it might even help you get out of this mess somewhat unscathed." He sat down and again pointed to the other chair at the kitchen table. "So, come on. I'd suggest you just give me a few minutes. What better options do you have here?"

Ryan hesitated, then sat down at the kitchen table.

"That chat just now, that wasn't Doom98," Agent Marcus explained.

"But you probably figured that out already. Unfortunately a little late. That was a colleague. Your buddy Doom98 is in custody."

Ryan's eyes widened.

"And you, he screwed you over," the agent continued. "For years now. We have the chat logs, we know what he told you, about 'staying clean' and all that. But you know what he did?"

He opened the briefcase, pulled out a folder, and tossed it casually on the table as if he were dealing cards. "Here, take a look at this."

Ryan reached for the folder tentatively, like he was afraid the contents might bite him.

When he looked inside, his breath caught in his throat. He didn't understand everything it said, but what he did understand was enough.

Doom98 had turned his hacking into big business. He had traded credit card numbers and passwords, installed spyware, blackmailed people with nude photos or confidential documents stolen from their hard drives... in short, he had done everything he had always warned Ryan not to do.

And to make matters worse, Ryan recognized some of the methods described there. Doom98 had exploited vulnerabilities that he himself, Ryan, had discovered and taught him!

"I... I didn't know anything about this!" he gasped.

The FBI agent shook his head in disapproval. "Well, well, well. If I were you, I'd probably wait until your parents and a lawyer get here. Just let me do the talking, OK?"

Ryan nodded.

"But just so you don't worry unnecessarily, we know you weren't directly involved in those things. We were able to reconstruct some of your hacks from the chat logs. And what can I say? Kudos, kid! You're good. If we hadn't caught Doom98, we never would have caught up with you."

Ryan was really confused. Now this guy was actually singing his praises?

"And we also discovered that you always followed Doom98's advice: aside from hacking into the systems, don't do anything illegal. In other words, you haven't done anything stupid."

Agent Marcus's expression became serious. "However, the whole thing still falls under cybercrime. And we could also charge you with aiding and abetting Doom98's crimes. Yes, I know it wasn't your intention, but you did provide him with the tools. Without you, many of his crimes would not have been possible. You could be looking at more than ten years in jail."

Ryan swallowed hard. He was shocked.

Marcus noticed his nervousness and smiled reassuringly. "But like I said, we recognize that you have talent, and that's why we want to make you an offer. You don't have to say anything right now, you can discuss it with your parents and your lawyer, but I just want you to know about it."

"You want me to testify against Doom98?" Ryan asked, his voice hoarse.

"No need. He hasn't covered his tracks nearly as well as you have. We have everything we need to put him on trial. No, we have a different proposition: we need people like you. If you agree to work for us from now on, we'll put in a good word for you with the district attorney."

Ryan didn't know what to say. An hour ago, his biggest worry had been whether he'd studied enough for tomorrow's history test. And now he had an FBI man sitting in front of him offering him a deal to keep him out of jail.

Agent Marcus stood up. "It's OK, you don't have to answer right away. Talk it over with your parents and your lawyer and then let me know."

Continue reading on page 131.

Ryan shook his head. "The story about the dashes in every line was a ploy. Reginald Dash's clue was far more creative."

Sarah frowned and studied the safe again.

Not a bad attempt, but go back to page 036 and try again. Could it have something to do with the way the name is written?

"Is everything OK?"

It took Ryan a moment to snap out of his memories.

"Is everything OK?" Sarah asked again. She looked a little worried.

Ryan nodded dismissively. "Yeah, fine. I just got distracted for a second."

The opening in the wall was now almost big enough to squeeze through. Ryan widened it a little more, but when he tried to climb through, Sarah held him back.

"Let's see what's waiting for us in there first." She shined her light through the hole in the wall and let out a surprised whistle. "Wow – *classy*!"

Following her gaze, Ryan understood what she meant. Behind the wall was an elegantly furnished room, probably in the same style as the whole speakeasy had been in its day. But unlike the front, there was no sign of vandalism. Everything was still in its place, as if time had stood still.

The pictures were still on the walls, and intact tables and chairs were scattered around the room, with a strangely jumbled collection of objects on them.

Ryan hesitated. It looked like... yes, the objects actually had numbers on them! He felt oddly familiar with the scene – as if he had just seen it, but from a different perspective. "Give me the notebook, please," he asked Sarah.

She handed it to him and he began to leaf through it.

"I think I know what you're looking for. It's toward the back," she said.

It took Ryan just moments to find the right page. There was a picture with a verse underneath it.

You need three numbers? Have you checked
The points where colors intersect?
Each color has a matching pair;
Extend their lines and see what's there.
But don't look from the side – instead,
Regard the view from overhead.
So what's the order? Simply use
The standard sequence of the hues.

Ryan looked down at the floor. There, right in front of the opening in the wall, was a small cross carved into the wooden floorboards, as if to mark a particularly important place. Ryan stood on it and looked around the room – and already had an idea how they would solve the mystery.

Study the pictures on the next two pages carefully. Then follow the instructions in the verse – and you'll have the code.

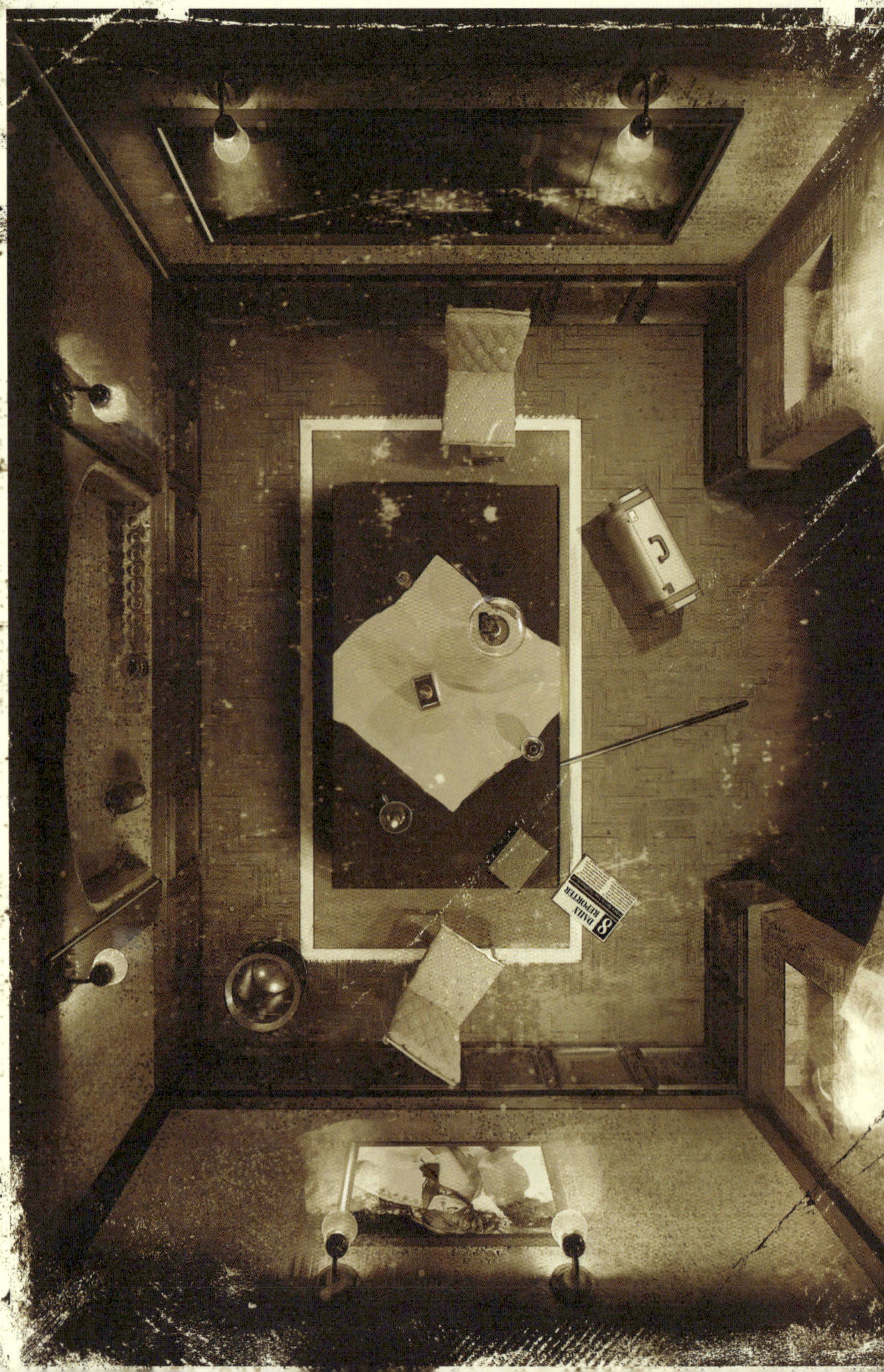
8
DAILY
REPORTER

When Ryan stepped out of the door and into the parking lot, he was met with dry heat. The weather forecast had announced a high of ninety-five degrees. It was probably even warmer here, with the lack of shade and the hot asphalt.

Sometimes Ryan missed the milder climate of the East Coast. But he didn't regret moving here. There was a lot he didn't like about the Midwest – most people didn't share his political views, and science and education often had a hard time competing with the prevailing religious beliefs. But at least there was open debate. Everyone knew where they stood with each other. He was fine with that, in contrast to the experiences he'd had in his previous line of work.

His house was quite small by local standards, but it was big enough for him. The only question was how long it would be sufficient for the books Ryan was accumulating. It already seemed as if every available wall was fitted with a shelf.

Ryan wasn't shy about telling people he didn't like the internet, and he meant it. Encyclopedias and reference books took the place that Google and Wikipedia would have filled. They might not always be up to date, but Ryan deliberately stayed away from the day-to-day developments in cryptography. He preferred to focus on the fundamentals – and those fundamentals had the convenient quality of remaining constant.

But he knew he couldn't maintain this online abstinence in the long run. Even now, he had to break it from time to time – to upload assignments to the school server, for example. But he was still able to keep his time online to a minimum.

He spent the next few hours preparing lessons for the coming days. Teachers were always said to have a lot of free time. Ryan couldn't say he agreed.

At some point, he felt he had earned a break. It was late enough to relax without feeling guilty, but still too early to prepare dinner. Ryan sat down at the kitchen table with a cup of coffee and took out the strange letter. Although he had no illusions about its contents, puzzles were his passion. And an unsolved mystery was like an itch waiting to be scratched.

He looked at the symbols again. At first glance, it looked like a classic substitution cipher. This type of encryption had been used since ancient times: each letter was replaced with a different symbol. It was very easy to hack, at least if you could guess what language the encrypted text was written in. This was because, in every language, certain letters occurred more frequently than others. This meant that common symbols almost certainly corresponded to common characters – and once you had managed to match up a few of them, you could easily work out the first syllables and word fragments.

This worked best with longer texts, because the higher the number of characters, the closer their frequencies came to their statistical averages. Short notes like this one might well have an unusually high number of rare letters, due to an unusual name, or something like that. Still, it was worth a try – if only because Ryan knew the frequencies of the most important letters by heart, anyway.

He took a sheet of paper and began to tally each individual character, starting by matching the most frequently appearing symbol with the letter E, the most common letter in many Western alphabets, then trying other likely pairings. But no clear picture emerged from the values, and the character distribution didn't make sense.

So it wasn't quite as straightforward as he had thought, Ryan was pleased to discover. It was rare enough that the creators of these puzzles put in more than the bare minimum of effort, despite the fact that when it came to solving these messages, the journey was the destination. He took a closer look at the encrypted message.

Some of the symbols looked familiar, although right then he couldn't think where he'd seen them before.

Ryan brooded. Theoretically, there were a number of ways the text could have been encoded, but most of them were unlikely in practice – they were just too good. Not *impossible* to crack, but too difficult for the average person at home.

The letter had been sent to him deliberately – in other words, someone wanted him to decode it. That was generally the major difference between puzzles and codes: a code was designed to be as secure as possible, so that ideally it could only be converted to plain text if you knew the right key. A puzzle, on the other hand, was designed to be solved. It came with its own key, so to speak. No matter how complicated it might seem, there were always hidden clues to the solution somewhere. If you found and used them, the rest would work itself out.

And if none of those clues could be found in the text itself, then he had to look for them elsewhere....

No doubt the symbols look familiar to you as well. Where have you seen them before? Why don't you look for them in the book? Then find the right spin to solve the puzzle.

076

"The combination was written right on it?" Smith asked incredulously. "I expected a little more imagination from Mr. Dash. Go on, open the safe!"

With trembling hands, Ryan set the numbers on the combination lock, fully aware that a gun was aimed at him.

The lock clicked, Ryan turned the handle of the safe – and the door remained locked! "It won't open!" shouted Ryan. "The combination was wrong!" He tugged at the door to demonstrate.

Smith cursed. "Hector! Check it!" he ordered his bodyguard.

Ryan had to press himself against the wall of the pit as the massive man jumped in beside him and began fumbling with the lock.

"He's telling the truth," said Hector, finally confirming what Ryan had said before climbing back out.

Smith's finger played with the trigger of the revolver. "You knew that, Creed, didn't you? Even I realized that a solution like that would be too easy. Come on now! If that safe isn't opened soon, I see no reason to bother with you and your friend any longer!"

Ryan swallowed hard and turned back to the vault.

Well, I guess that didn't work. Go back to page 125
and try again. Here's a hint: maybe
Dash's name speaks for itself?

077

They waited in silence. It wasn't the right atmosphere for small talk. After a minute or two, Ryan heard a muffled elevator bell from near the exit. Moments later, the metal door opened and a tall, bald, pale-skinned man emerged. He wore an expensive watch on one wrist and carried a small metal case in his other hand.

Ryan estimated the man to be in his late fifties. He was wearing a suit that only at second glance betrayed how expensive it must have been. Nothing about the jacket and pants screamed *I'm expensive*, but – and this was much harder to achieve – they were immaculate, fitting as discreetly and perfectly as only true professionals could tailor.

This had to be the man who went by the name of "Will Power." And although he obviously had plenty of money, Ryan had never seen his face before. Not surprising, given that there were plenty of rich people all over America who had made their fortunes without attracting much public attention.

"Mr. Creed," Power said. His voice sounded benignly amused. "Sarah told me there were some problems. How can I help?"

"Well, perhaps by finally explaining to me what's going on. You may enjoy leaving me twisting in the wind all this time, but I want to know what it is you want from me."

"First of all, I don't want *anything* from you. Instead, I want to give you something."

Power pulled a checkbook from his pocket and began writing.

Ryan shook his head. "What kind of welcome...? Do you really think you can *buy* me, Mr. Power – or whatever your real name is? Let me tell you something: if money was important to me, I wouldn't have become a college lecturer."

Power had finished writing and put the pen back in his pocket. "I know. That's why I'm offering this money not to you, but to your foundation."

He tore the check from the checkbook and showed it to Ryan. It was, in fact, made out to the Foundation – and for a substantial sum. Significantly more than the total donations received to date.

"You don't think I believe you brought me here only to hand me a check, do you?"

"Not *only* that, Mr. Creed, but this has always been part of my intention. This money will go to your foundation if you solve a little puzzle for me right here and now. And if you work for me for a few days after that, it will be considerably more. Many times more."

"*Work* for you? And what exactly does that entail?"

"One thing at a time. Solve the puzzle, then we'll talk – and you can decide if you wish to accept the assignment." Power pointed at Sarah Corbet. "Of course, you may decide not to accept my donation and have Sarah take you back to the airport immediately. I would regret that very much, but I would not stop you. It is entirely up to you."

Ryan cursed inwardly. The guy still hadn't said a word about what this was all about. Instead, he dangled a bait so big that it was almost impossible not to bite.

No matter what Ryan had told Power, of *course* he would have had a hard time saying no, even if the money was meant for him. He might be an idealist, but he wasn't completely immune to the lure of wealth. And turning down a donation like this for the Foundation was another matter entirely.

He thought of all the clients Jamie represented. Ordinary people who'd had the misfortune to find themselves on the wrong side of a bad cop or prosecutor. People in the legal system should care about truth and justice, but some care more about their own careers – or maybe they're just power-hungry assholes who think the rules only apply to others, not themselves.

It was entirely possible that this Power was also an asshole – his actions so far (and his ridiculously arrogant alias) certainly suggested that. But if he was, at least he was someone who wanted to give money to a good cause in exchange for Ryan's willingness to look at a puzzle. Could he – no, *did* he – even have the *right* to refuse?

"Fine." Ryan sighed. "On one condition: afterwards, you finally explain to me exactly what the deal is here."

Sarah Corbet smiled triumphantly. "Like I said, everyone is impressed by money."

Power, meanwhile, remained unmoved. "A very good decision, Mr. Creed. And yes, I assure you that once you have solved this riddle, I will answer all your questions. Both about the riddle and about my assignment for you. And should you not be completely satisfied with what you learn, you may simply take the check and fly back home."

Power opened the case and took out a clear envelope containing a yellowed, handwritten sheet of paper with a few coins stuck to it. “Please handle this with care, Mr. Creed. It’s a valuable original. More valuable than you can imagine.”

Ryan carefully took the sheet and placed it on the hood of the SUV. Up close he noticed a faint checkered pattern on the paper.

Can you decipher the code of the coins? You might want to take a closer look at the dates on them. Three of them have dates that may look familiar to you. Some information elsewhere on the page may also be helpful.

Dear Stuart, August 15, 1934

I don't know when you will read this.
I will probably be dead by then.
But I'm sure that you will be able to decipher the
code of the three coins without me.
Together with the map, it will show you the way.

With love,
Your father, Reginald.

082

"Madison Street," Ryan read, after solving the riddle in the notes. "And the riddle in the letter resulted in a series of numbers: 635. Probably the house number then!"

"Sounds logical," Power said. "But don't assume you'll find the coins there. Reginald Dash was known for his eccentricities. He wouldn't have made it that easy."

Ryan stood. "How far is that address from here?"

"Madison Street is a little farther south. You can get there in a few minutes by car." Power looked at his watch. "And I think your ride should be here any minute."

As if on cue, the elevator bell rang. As the doors opened, Sarah Corbet stepped out in a completely different outfit. Instead of business attire, she was wearing rugged outdoor clothing: jeans, a functional vest with lots of pockets, and boots with thick soles.

"I'm ready," she declared, "Do we have a solution yet?"

Power nodded. "Pioneer Square. 635 Madison Street."

"Let's go then," Corbet announced.

Power handed the book to Corbet. "Take good care of it. It's one of a kind."

Ryan looked out the window. The sun was already low over the waters of Puget Sound. "All right, then. Let's see how much we can get done tonight."

Power stayed behind in the office. *No surprise there*, Ryan thought. He had spent a lot of money to secure support. So why should he get involved himself?

083

Ryan wasn't sure he'd actually get the money he'd been promised for the Foundation. But at least he already had the check – and now he was actually starting to feel tempted by the whole thing. A hidden treasure of gold – who could resist?

Once in the car, Sarah Corbet offered to ease back on the formalities. "We're going to be working together nonstop for the next few days. We can be on a first-name basis, right? You can call me Sarah."

Ryan accepted.

He looked at Sarah's clothes. "You look like you're going on a wilderness expedition."

"Look around you! The wilderness is right around the corner. Go twenty miles in any direction and you're in the middle of the mountains." She thought for a moment. "OK, not exactly *any* direction. Twenty miles *west* and you're at the bottom of the *ocean*."

Sarah had brought Dash's notebook from the office. Ryan flipped through it. It was full of mysterious instructions and diagrams.

"And you're sure that the way to the location isn't simply hidden somewhere in this book?" he asked.

"Absolutely sure. We've been looking at it for weeks – and it always seems like you only have pieces of a puzzle in front of you. I don't think we can solve the puzzles with this book alone – but not without it either."

Ryan studied the book carefully. "That means this little thing is worth a couple hundred million. I hope you made a backup."

"Oh, Will had it photographed immediately, but it may well be that not all the information was saved. It's possible that Dash has hidden some clues that can only be found in this original."

Ryan's fingers involuntarily tightened around the old notebook. It dawned on him that he had probably never held anything so rare and valuable before.

They left the central business district behind. The houses grew older and the elevations lower, and soon the road led them past red brick buildings from the late nineteenth century.

"This neighborhood is called Pioneer Square," Sarah explained. "It's where Seattle was born. Later, the center moved a little bit to the north, where the skyscrapers are. Many of these buildings were here in Reginald Dash's time." Sarah turned on her blinkers and pulled to the side of the road. They got out of the car.

"Number 635 must be a little farther down there," Sarah explained, pointing west.

They followed the street, passing old and new buildings, until they finally reached 635 Madison Street. Or at least where it should have been. The whole building had been demolished!

"I guess this is it," Ryan muttered, shaking his head. "Looks like we're a few years too late."

Sarah took the map out of the notebook and checked their position.

"Yes. The address should be right here."

The light from the streetlamps fell on blades of grass swaying in the wind.

Ryan was a little disappointed, and not just because of the money. He had begun to look forward to the next puzzle. And now they were standing at a barren lot.

"Should we call Power or do you want to tell him in person?" he asked Sarah.

But Sarah didn't pay any attention to him, instead staring intently at the map. Then she burst out laughing: "Reginald Dash was really good! He almost fooled us!" She held the notebook out to Ryan and pointed to a small notation on the edge of the map: *Planning Status: May 1889*. "Well, does that tell you anything?"

Ryan shook his head. "Do you think there's some kind of code hidden in the date?"

"In a way, yes, but not like in your puzzles! Reginald Dash was making use of the city's history."

"I'm just going to nod as if I understand what you mean."

Sarah pointed at the buildings around them. "Notice anything? They're all brick – and all from the late nineteenth century."

Ryan still didn't know what she was getting at. "That was the norm back then."

"Yes, it was! But Seattle is a few decades older. Yet here, in the oldest part of town, there are *no* houses from the actual founding years. And do you know why?"

"They were torn down?" Ryan guessed.

"Almost," Sarah replied. "Most of them *burned* down. In a big fire that practically destroyed the whole town, because it was all constructed of wood. And we learned the date in history class: June 6, 1889."

Ryan looked at the map. "So the map shows the town before the fire." He paused, confused. "But what's that all about? Dash hid the coins sometime after 1933. Why would he put an old map like that in there?"

"It's a clue," Sarah explained. "After the fire, the town was rebuilt in these brick houses. And since everything was ruined, anyway, the town fathers made another change while they were at it: the town was raised by one floor."

"What do you mean?"

"Well, old Seattle often had to deal with flooding when Puget Sound got a little rough. That's why they backfilled the ground when they rebuilt it, to keep everyone's feet dry."

"It's great that you're giving me a lesson in urban history, but I still don't understand how this is going to help us find the coins."

"This is where it gets interesting! It takes time to backfill an entire neighborhood. They couldn't do it right after the fire. So at first, the people rebuilt their houses where they had stood before. But they knew that the ground would be raised later! Therefore, they built the second floor of their buildings to later become the first floor."

087

Ryan looked at the old buildings around them. They looked pretty ordinary – reddish brick houses with three or four floors. "Wait a minute! Are you saying that we're actually standing in front of the second floor of these houses?"

"Exactly. And the ground floor is actually *under*ground."

He pointed to the wasteland. "So you think there might be a remnant of the old house here under the grass?"

Sarah nodded. "And what we're looking for is definitely on that level. That's why Reginald Dash used such an old plan."

"And how are we going to *get* to it? We can't really dig up the site to look for the old foundations."

"You've met Will," Sarah replied dryly. "It wouldn't be a problem for him."

Ryan was surprised. "Seriously? You're going to get a construction crew?"

Sarah grinned. "I don't think that will be necessary. We can make this easier."

She walked off, motioning for Ryan to follow her.

"The old streets weren't completely filled in back then," Sarah explained as they walked toward an intersection. She pointed to some glass bricks set into the sidewalk. "See those? Those are skylights for underground passageways."

"Underground passages?!" Ryan repeated incredulously. "Are you serious?"

"Yes," Sarah confirmed. "For a few decades, there were actually two levels to the city around here. At some point, the lower level was abandoned and forgotten about."

The intersection turned out to be a small tree-lined square flanked by old buildings. If it weren't for the noise of the nearby highway, Ryan might have thought he was in a sleepy backwater instead of one of the region's most important cities.

"Meanwhile," Sarah continued, "the old passageways are anything but forgotten."

She walked to a narrow storefront with a large sign on the door: *Seattle Underground Tours – Daily 10:00 a.m. to 6:00 p.m.*

"It's a tourist attraction now?" Ryan didn't like the sound of that. With crowds of people squeezing through the corridors every day, there was a real danger that there wouldn't be much left of whatever Reginald Dash had hidden down there.

Sarah didn't share his skepticism. "As long as we haven't seen with our own eyes that there's nothing there, I trust that good old Mr. Dash planned his stash to be future-proof."

Ryan sighed. "All right, then, we can take a tour in the morning."

Sarah pulled something out of her bag and fumbled with the lock on the shop door. "Why wait so long?" she asked, pushing the door open.

Ryan took a step back. "Wait! You want to break in? Power guaranteed me we'd be completely legal."

089

“Don’t *be* like that – we’re not robbing a bank or anything. We’re just looking around at a different time than people usually do. If it makes you feel better, we can leave a few dollars on the counter to cover the entrance fee.”

Ryan looked around. Were they being watched? A white SUV drove slowly past the square, but the driver didn’t seem to be paying any attention to them; rather, he seemed to be looking for a particular street. A moment later, he made a turn and the car disappeared around a corner. Ryan breathed a sigh of relief.

Sarah laughed. “I don’t believe it! You’re *the* Ryan Creed, aren’t you? The prodigy who hacked into high-security servers back in the day. I *am* remembering this correctly, right?”

Ryan rolled his eyes. He didn’t like it when his past was brought up. “Yeah,” he admitted. “But that was *ages* ago.”

“Twelve years,” Sarah countered. “At most. I bet you still have to show your driver’s license to buy beer now, don’t you?”

“I’ve changed my mind about a lot of things since then,” Ryan insisted.

“I’m not buying it. As a teenager, you hacked into super-secure computers, and now you’re scared shitless to look around some tourist trap at night!”

Ryan thought for a moment. Actually, Sarah was right. Compared to the things he had done in the past, this was harmless. Still, it made him uneasy.

“It’s a matter of principle,” he finally explained. “First it’s ‘*nothing illegal*,’ and now we’re breaking in here. What’s next?”

"Oh, *I* see! Afraid that trespassing might be your gateway drug?" Sarah smiled. "Don't worry, it really won't get any more illegal than this. We might look around a few places we weren't invited to, but that's it. No murder or manslaughter, no theft, and no hostages. Can you live with that?"

Ryan relented. "All right, then. The sign here says, *Visit us!* So... let's do what they say."

As they entered the deserted lobby, Sarah dropped a few dollar bills into the tip jar. "There you go. As promised."

Ryan watched as she expertly manipulated her lockpick to relock the outer door.

"Looks pretty professional," he commented.

"When you work for Will, it can come in handy to acquire some unusual skills." She walked past the ticket booth to a staircase leading down. "All right, let's head underground."

The steps were quite steep, and for reasons of security, Sarah and Ryan hadn't turned on any lights. Their descent was illuminated only by Sarah's flashlight.

In less than ten feet, they reached the end of the stairs and Sarah pointed the flashlight forward. They were standing in a low basement room with solid brick walls. The beam of light illuminated pictures, display boards, and exhibits that told the story of the Seattle Underground, but there was no exit.

"Try behind us," Ryan suggested.

Sarah turned around. Sure enough, behind them, right where the entrance was one floor up, was a wall of old windows that had long since been boarded up. Between them, an archway led into the darkness.

091

"Bingo!" Sarah whispered. "Welcome to Seattle Underground."

Continue reading on page 050.

092

"I know the way!" Ryan finally announced. "If you follow me, I'll get you out of here. But like I said, only if you get rid of your weapons first."

Smith looked at Ryan's coal notes on the floor, which seemed to indicate a way through the maze of tunnels. "I could just leave you here and go."

"You could," Ryan admitted. "But first, you wouldn't have any help finding the coins, and second, you don't know if I haven't worked an error into the drawing. It's up to you if you want to take that risk."

Smith signaled to Hector. "Tie their hands! And take their phones."

Hector had zip ties with him. The sharp plastic cut into Ryan's flesh, and he watched as Sarah reluctantly allowed herself to be bound as well.

The bodyguard was taken aback when he saw Ryan's old-fashioned phone with its keypad and black-and-white display.

"What?" asked Ryan. "It does everything I need it to do!"

Hector grumbled, shook his head, and resumed his duties.

When he was done, Smith checked the fit of their restraints. "OK. Then I'll hold up my end of the bargain, too."

Smith threw his gun into a corner of the cave and motioned for Hector to do the same. The bodyguard obeyed immediately. Questioning or doubting his boss didn't seem to be part of his job description.

"Come on, then, Mr. Creed. Get us out of this damned place!"

093

The walk was long and the tunnels narrow; in some places, Ryan's shoulders touched the walls on both sides. He had no idea how the muscular Hector had managed to get through here.

It wasn't easy for him to keep his bearings in this maze of passages and remember the route the map had indicated. Ryan came close to making a few wrong turns, but always realized at the last moment.

He had no way of knowing exactly how long they had been wandering through the mine. It was hard to tell the time without daylight. But at last he saw something glittering in the glare of the flashlights: the tracks of the mine cart! And a moment later he recognized the intersection where they had begun their descent into the mine.

"A left here and we'll be back outside in no time!" he announced.

And indeed, minutes later they saw daylight streaming in from the mouth of the cave.

By then it was afternoon, and Ryan saw that a second helicopter had landed not far from Sarah's. Smith's transport, he guessed. A man in an olive jumpsuit sat in the cockpit, his eyes closed in relaxation. When he heard the group coming out of the mine, he got out and drew a pistol.

Ryan stood still. "Tell him to throw the gun away," he reminded Smith.

Smith sighed and gave the order. "You heard him, Gus."

Unlike Hector, Gus was apparently capable of thinking for himself. Confused, he looked at his boss, who confirmed the order. "Go on, do it!"

Perplexed, Gus shrugged and tossed the gun.

"Let's find out what Mr. Dash has prepared for us now," Smith muttered, opening the metal box they had found in the mine.

Inside was a folded piece of paper. Gently, Smith lifted it out and read the dedication: "'For Stuart Dash. With love, Your father Reginald.'" Smith laughed. "I think we're getting close!" He unfolded the document and smiled triumphantly. "I knew it!" Ryan looked at it. It was a map.

"Does this mean anything to you, Gus?" Smith asked the pilot.

Gus studied the map for a moment. "That looks like Copper Lake, sir," he said.

"Wonderful! Do you know if it's possible to land there?"

"Yes, sir."

"Then let's get going!"

Although Smith's helicopter was a bit roomier than the one Sarah had flown, it was still very cramped inside. Smith and Gus sat in the front seats, while Ryan and Sarah had to squeeze into the back seat next to the bulky Hector.

The noise of the rotors made it impossible to have a conversation during the flight. But that didn't mean Ryan and Sarah couldn't communicate.

Ryan waited until Hector was staring out the window, bored, then he looked at Sarah and mouthed the words "*Copper Lake,*" trying to look as questioning as possible. *Do you know where that is?* he wanted to convey.

Sarah understood. She nodded weakly, then briefly grimaced in frustration.

Copper Lake was a long way from civilization, Ryan assumed, and therefore a long way from any help.

And true, the peaks around them were getting higher and higher. Here and there they were already covered with snow. Ryan could make out fewer and fewer signs of human habitation in the valleys below.

"*National Park*," Sarah mouthed.

Ryan cursed under his breath – because that meant not only untouched nature, but also extreme isolation.

Finally, the monotonous drone of the rotors changed, and as Ryan looked out the window, he realized they were approaching a lake. Copper Lake, he assumed.

Gus was hovering just above the water, heading for a flat, wide-open spot on the shore, some kind of gravel beach.

The helicopter touched down softly on the rocks.

As Ryan disembarked, he was struck by how beautiful this place was. The lake was surrounded by densely wooded slopes and snow-capped peaks that reflected almost perfectly on the smooth surface of the water.

A paradise, Ryan thought – at least for anyone not currently in the hands of criminals.

Meanwhile, Smith had unrolled the map again and pointed to it. "We're here – and it looks like we have to get over *there.*"

He pointed in the direction of a short pier, then folded the map back up before Ryan could take a closer look.

The group set off. Ryan and Sarah walked slowly. They didn't want to risk tripping, which might prove extremely painful with their hands tied.

"Do you really think the coins are here?" Sarah whispered to him.

"I have no idea. The dedication certainly makes it sound that way." Ryan carefully climbed over a log on the path in front of him.

"And if they are, who's to say Smith will keep his word and release us afterwards?" She looked around. "If he kills us here, no one will find us. And if he just leaves us here, they still won't find us."

Ryan nodded grimly. This didn't bode well for them.

"Shut up and move!" Hector intimidatingly brandished a shovel he had brought from the helicopter.

Continue reading on page 111.

097

Half an hour later, Sarah pulled into the driveway of a small motel on the outskirts of town whose flickering neon sign promised "air conditioning and cable TV in all rooms."

"Power made a reservation for me *here*?" Ryan was surprised.

"No, but I can't take you to your hotel. It's too risky. Will always has his guests stay there. If those guys who followed us know about it, they might be waiting for us there. That's why it's better for us to stay here tonight." She got out and gestured to the back seat. "Don't forget your stuff."

Ryan grabbed the bags and followed Sarah. "Wait, why did you say *those guys*? We only saw the one car – what makes you think there's a whole conspiracy behind it that knows all about Will?"

"Because it's about money, Ryan. A *lot* of money. You should always assume the worst."

The teenage receptionist barely looked up from his cell phone game when they inquired about a room.

Soon after, Ryan set down his shopping bags in the simply furnished but clean room on the first floor. Looking around, he saw that everything looked just like the motel rooms he had stayed in on countless trips: worn carpeting, plywood furniture in a design that might have been fashionable thirty years ago, and a clunky AC unit rattling away by the window.

He turned it off – it was already cool enough.

Sarah came in. She had moved the car.

"And you're *sure* those guys won't find us here?" asked Ryan.

"It's dark, and the car is parked where it can't be seen from the street. I don't think they'll be able to check all the hotel parking lots in Seattle by tomorrow morning."

She pointed to the bed. "I'll take the side by the door, if you don't mind."

"Yeah, sure." Ryan hesitated for a moment. "And you're OK with us sleeping in the same bed?"

Sarah laughed. "So far I have the impression that you are a gentleman. But just in case I'm wrong, let me warn you: I know judo and karate."

Ryan joined in with her laughter and shrugged. "Don't worry, I'll be on my best behavior."

The day had been exhausting and they headed straight to bed. Once the lights were out, another thought occurred to Ryan. "Say, what exactly do you know about me? You and Power?"

"Everything that can be found in public sources. The newspaper reports about your trial back then, that you worked for the authorities, and so on. Why?"

"Well, isn't that kind of unfair? That you know so much and I don't know anything?"

Sarah's voice sharpened a bit. "If you think I'm going to tell you my life story, I'm sorry, but that's *not* going to happen. You of *all* people should know how important privacy can be."

Ryan was a little surprised by her harsh tone. Had he hit a nerve? He decided it would be better not to probe any further for now.

"No, I was thinking more about Will Power. What's it like working for him?"

Sarah thought for a moment. "Will is filthy rich, you've already figured *that* out. And he's not a bad person. When he promises you something, he keeps his word. No tricks or hidden excuses. But he's also an egotist – I doubt he'd have gotten so rich otherwise."

"What do you mean by that?"

"Unless he's made some other promise to you, Will will always think of himself first. If there's something in it for you and me, that's fine with him, but we're *way* down on his list of priorities." She paused and thought for a moment. "I guess what I'm trying to say is that this kind of assignment from Will might be a great opportunity – but still, don't forget to look out for yourself."

"Sounds exhausting," Ryan said.

"That's just the way it is. Life is always stressful," Sarah replied. "You just have to get your priorities straight so you know what you're striving for." With that, she wished Ryan a good night and rolled over to her other side.

For a few moments, Ryan lay awake, staring at the ceiling, wondering how many of his priorities in life Will and Sarah shared. He suspected there weren't many.

Ryan was exhausted, but his day had been too exciting to fall asleep right away.

100 AYL

Sarah's visit to the college in the morning. The flight to Seattle. The strange man who called himself "Will Power." Searching the Seattle Underground. And, of course, the guys who had followed them.

None of this seemed to bother Sarah. The regularity of her breathing indicated that she was already asleep. Meanwhile, Ryan's mind drifted back to the past....

== E-RazOr has joined the channel.
<Doom98> @E-RazOr Hi! How's it going?
<E-RazOr> I screwed up!
<Doom98> Stop! Not here!

A moment later there was a ping. The chat program indicated that a private message for Ryan had come in:

== Doom98 has invited you to a private chat session. Will you accept? (Y/N)

Frantically, Ryan typed "Y" and a new chat window opened.

== E-RazOr has joined the private chat.
== Doom98 has joined the private chat.
<Doom98> What's up?!
<E-RazOr> I screwed up.
<Doom98> You already said that. Screwed up how, man?!
<E-RazOr> My VPN went down and I didn't notice.
<Doom98> Shit!

<Doom98> What were you doing at the time?

<E-RazOr> Was just before an action.

<Doom98> BEFORE an action or DURING?

<E-RazOr> The script didn't run long. 20, 30 seconds maybe.

<Doom98> That's forever! Were you at least on Tor?

<E-RazOr> Nope. Crashed along with the VPN.

<Doom98> Man! What did I teach you? VPN and Tor are like condoms! They prevent unpleasant surprises once you get inside!

<Doom98> Now any admin can see your IP in their log files. And if they call the cops, you're screwed.

<E-RazOr> I know. Shit, shit, shit! My parents will kill me if the cops show up here!

<Doom98> Should have thought of that before.

<E-RazOr> Shut up! What the hell am I supposed to do now?

<Doom98> Relax! What's the IP of the server you were going for?

<E-RazOr> 198.51.100.27

<E-RazOr> It's a textile firm. Involved in child labor, I think.

<Doom98> Want to play Robin Hood?

<Doom98> Very bad idea.

<Doom98> I told you: greed makes you blind. If you're emotionally invested in the target, you make mistakes. No matter what you're after.

<Doom98> And I have to clean up the mess.

<E-RazOr> You mean you'll help me?!

<Doom98> Already done!

<Doom98> Went in through the laptop. Log file wiped clean, like you were never there.
<E-RazOr> Wow! Right on! THANKS.
<E-RazOr> You just saved my life! No kidding!
<Doom98> Just be more careful next time, yeah?
<Doom98> And remember, stay clean. Look around, have fun, but nothing more. No raids, no heroics, or you'll go down fast!
== Doom98 has left the private chat.

Ryan had learned his lesson back then. But he had also realized that when people are breathing down your neck, every mistake you make is a gift to them. That's why OpSec – Operational Security – had become his top priority. He configured his software to run only when the connection was fundamentally secure. Still, at every stage of a hack, he would check to make sure everything was working as it should.

He never wanted to experience anything like that night ever again.

He was sure that Sarah and this Will Power were serious about OpSec, too – they didn't seem like the kind of people to take unnecessary risks. And yet the guys in the white SUV had found them. That meant Sarah, Will, or himself had somehow slipped up despite all their caution, or they were up against an opponent from whom they could keep no secrets.

Under normal circumstances, this would have been something to lose sleep over. But by now Ryan was so tired that he passed out anyway, his thoughts still swirling.

Continue reading on page 047.

Ryan's jaw dropped. "*Thirty* coins?! That would be incredibly valuable!"

Power nodded. "That's why I'm willing to make an appropriate donation to your foundation. Would ten million dollars be a fair reimbursement for your help?"

Ryan was speechless. Power's first check had been generous – but ten *million?* That would fundamentally change the Foundation's work!

Power drummed his fingers on the desk. "I'll take your silence as a 'yes,' Mr. Creed. Is that correct?"

"And there's nothing illegal about it?" asked Ryan.

"Not in the least. As far as I'm concerned, once this is over, you can tell the authorities and the world about it. But I must ask you to be discreet during your search; we don't want to attract any copycats."

That sounded reasonable to Ryan. "And you're *sure* I'm the right person to find these coins?"

"In fact, I think you're the only one who can succeed," Power replied. "To put it bluntly, I don't fully expect you to find the coins. They may already be stolen or destroyed. But I do expect you to follow their trail as far as it leads. As soon as you guarantee me your cooperation, you may begin. And I'm pretty sure these puzzles will dwarf anything you've encountered before."

Ryan sighed. He knew that this was a once-in-a-lifetime opportunity. If he accepted, he might curse himself later. But if he didn't, he'd *certainly* curse himself for the rest of his life. And not just because of the money for the Foundation.

He held out his hand to Power. “Fine, I’m in.”

“Very well!” Power shook his hand. He opened one of the drawers in his desk and pulled out a well-worn notebook. The cover was monogrammed with the letters “R” and “D.”

“These are the writings of one Reginald Dash. He was a very active coin dealer in the 1930s, and there have always been rumors that he may have obtained some of the Double Eagles at that time. Most sources mention thirty pieces. So I’ve made it my mission to obtain as much of his collection as I can. The letter you deciphered earlier was written to his son, Stuart Dash. I assume he intended to leave the coins to him and wanted to keep them in a safe place until then. His papers contain clues as to where he deposited them.”

“And how can you be sure that Dash’s son hasn’t already moved them from where they were hidden?”

“Stuart died before Reginald Dash. He went down in the Pacific in 1943, on an aircraft carrier. Reginald had no other heirs. But there’s no record of him selling the coins elsewhere.”

“So you believe they’re still in their hiding place.”

106

"Correct. And I was fortunate enough to get my hands on this little book from Reginald Dash's possessions a few weeks ago." Power indicated the notebook. "And I'm fairly certain it points the way to the treasure. If only you can read it right... And that's where *you* come in, Mr. Creed."

"The letter mentioned a map. The numerical code and a map would show us the way."

Power opened the book. "I assume it's probably this map. A map of Seattle, the old downtown area."

Ryan examined the map more closely. There was text next to it:

Fold three lined pages to the right,
Then find the fourth line in plain sight.
Follow where the letters lead
To find coordinates to read,
Then let this order be your guide:
Top or bottom, then the side.

"Well, do you have any ideas?" asked Power expectantly.

What do you think? The text mentions "lined pages," so try looking for pages in the book that have unusual lines! Then relate what you find to the text and the map.

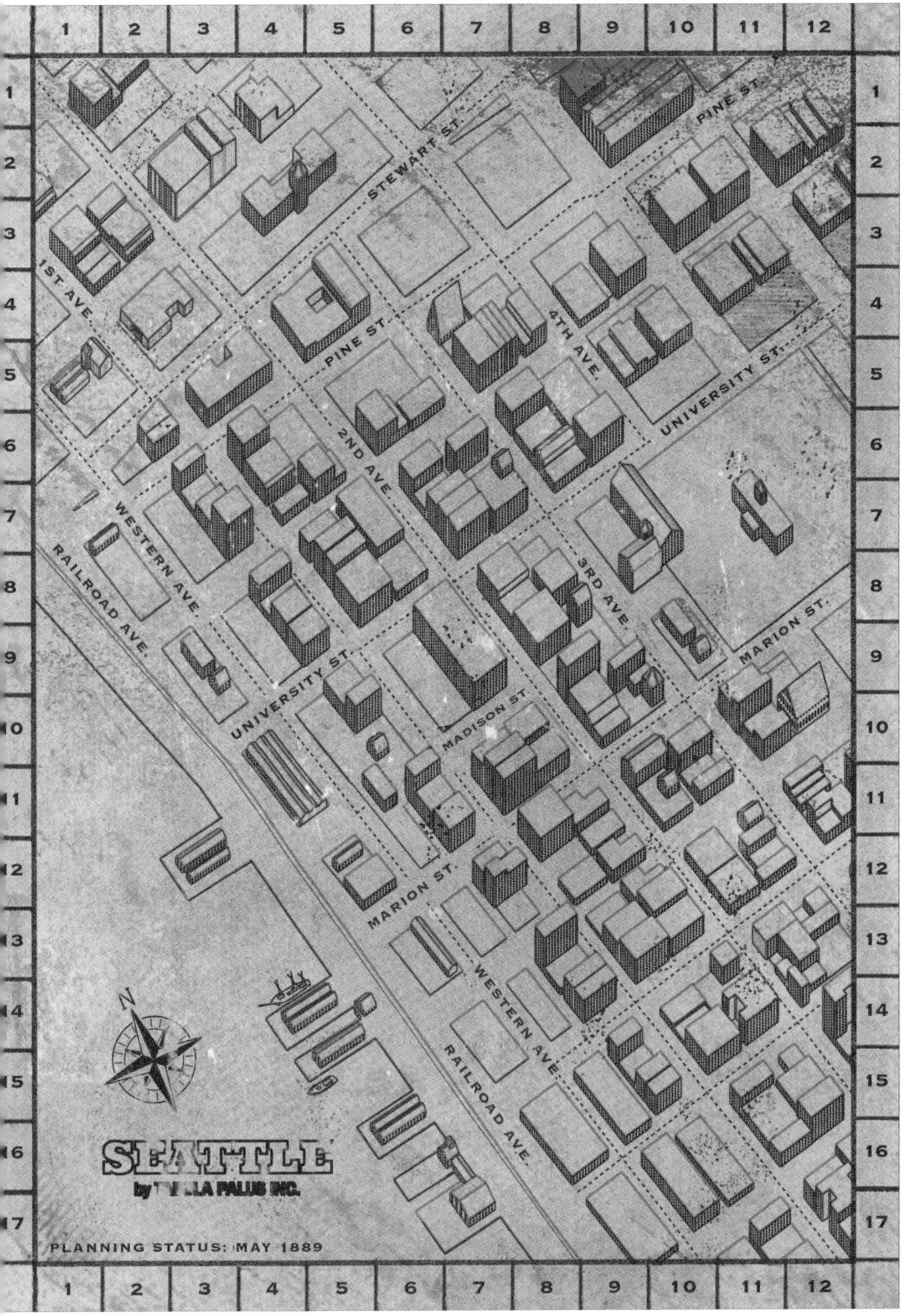
1 2 3 4 5 6 7 8 9 10 11 12
1 2 3 4 5 6 7 8 9 10 11 12 13 14 15 16 17
PINE ST.
STEWART ST.
1ST AVE.
PINE ST.
4TH AVE.
UNIVERSITY ST.
2ND AVE.
WESTERN AVE.
RAILROAD AVE.
3RD AVE.
MARION ST.
UNIVERSITY ST.
MADISON ST.
MARION ST.
WESTERN AVE.
RAILROAD AVE.
N
SEATTLE
PLANNING STATUS: MAY 1889

108

"There's something here!" Sarah shouted. "Something made of metal!"

The place Dash's instructions had led them was right next to one of the heavy supporting pillars.

Ryan crouched down beside Sarah and peered into the hole she had dug. The flashlight illuminated Reginald Dash's monogram on a metal plate. Engraved below it was a verse:

Friend, for your sake, I implore
Leave undisturbed what lies in store.
Lacking knowledge, at this depth,
One misstep and it's your last breath.

But if you'd finish what's begun,
Your next path lies beneath the sun.
Once you arrive where you've been led,
The answer will be on your head.
The symbols may appear abstract,
But they're your code: complete, intact.

"What is *that* supposed to mean?" Sarah wondered.

"I have no idea. But it sounds like there must be something more here. I mean, there's a warning about leaving something undisturbed."

"Sounds creepy. But I think we should keep digging anyway."

"Agreed," Ryan said. "Let's see what else Dash has prepared for us."

109

Ryan put the metal plate to the side and they continued to carefully work their way forward, Sarah with a small shovel from her vest, Ryan with his bare hands. He could feel the sting of small stones under his fingernails as he dug – and then, suddenly, something hard and cold.

"There's something here!" he exclaimed.

Sarah lowered her shovel, and together they uncovered an angular object.

"An iron bar," Sarah muttered disappointedly. "You think this is what we're looking for?"

Ryan tapped it. It sounded solid.

"Mmm, I don't know. There can't be anything hidden inside." He wiped some dirt off the metal. "Oh, but look!"

Sarah smiled. "Reginald Dash's monogram. The man really went to a lot of trouble..."

"So we're still on the right track," Ryan said.

They carefully exposed more of the metal bar. It turned out to be part of a complex construction, firmly embedded in the ground and looking more and more like...

"A cage!" Sarah exclaimed. "Dash built an underground cage here!"

"That suggests the contents might be of interest," Ryan replied. "And probably valuable."

"You think it's the coins?" Sarah asked.

"Let's put it this way: I can't think of many other reasons why someone would go through all this trouble."

But even as Ryan said it, doubts began to creep in. There was something about this cage that didn't sit right with him. He just couldn't put his finger on it.

110

The bars of the cage construction were just far enough apart for them to put their hands through and continue digging. It wasn't long before they came against another obstruction.

"It's not a bar this time." Ryan pushed the dirt aside, revealing something flat and angular underneath.

"A steel box!" Sarah exclaimed.

"Very nice!" a voice came from behind them. "Put your hands in the air! And turn around very slowly!"

Ryan and Sarah froze.

Continue reading on page 147.

The pier they were headed for was near a promontory that jutted out into the lake. The wood was quite old, and Ryan thought it was very likely that it was the same structure that had stood here in Reginald Dash's time. The blue rowboat tied to it, on the other hand, looked much newer.

The sight of it gave Ryan a brief glimmer of hope. At least this meant that the area wasn't completely deserted! If Smith was really letting them go, they could hope that at least the owner of this boat would show up at some point. Preferably before Ryan and Sarah fell victim to hunger, thirst, or wild animals.

He pushed the thought aside. He would think about that when the time came. And right now it wasn't at all clear if it would even come to that.

Smith unfolded the map again, then picked up Dash's notebook and flipped through it.

A moment later, he looked at Ryan smugly. "You see, I *am* a good student." He held the map out to Ryan and pointed to some symbols along the edge. "I figured out all by myself that these symbols are a clue to the notes."

"So, what do you want from me?" Ryan asked, annoyed. "A gold star?"

"No, I want what you promised: your assistance. Because the notes contain another riddle from our friend Reginald Dash, and that's *your* job again."

He put the map down and held the notebook in front of Ryan's face.

Ryan had an idea. "Wait a minute, that's not how it works!" he objected in a deliberately loud voice. "You can't expect me to work like this! I need my hands."

Smith looked at him with obvious annoyance. "That's not what we agreed on, Mr. Creed."

"The deal is that I will help you. Well, I would be happy to." Ryan tried to sound as convincing as he could. "But I need to have my hands free to solve the puzzle!"

Noticing Smith's skeptical look, he continued: "There are three of you here! There are only two of us, and Sarah is tied up. You and your people can easily keep an eye on me. And I bet your people have all the training they need to take me out if necessary."

Smith considered this, then made a dismissive hand gesture. "All right, if that's what it takes! Hector, cut the restraints! And keep an eye on him!"

Ryan breathed a sigh of relief. At least his hands were free again. It was a start.

When Hector cut the zip tie with a pocketknife, Ryan thanked him curtly. The bodyguard just grunted and pressed the tip of the knife menacingly against Ryan's back for a moment before folding it away again.

Ryan asked Smith for the map and notebook and turned his attention to Reginald Dash's next riddle.

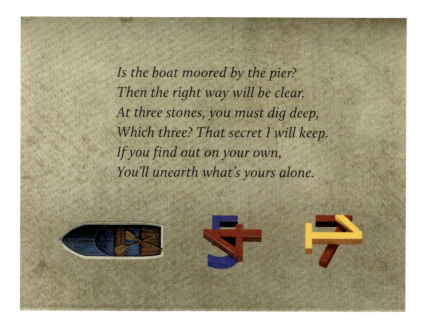

Is the boat moored by the pier?
Then the right way will be clear.
At three stones, you must dig deep,
Which three? That secret I will keep.
If you find out on your own,
You'll unearth what's yours alone.

Can you make sense of Reginald Dash's poem? You must have seen the little boat underneath it before. And what do the overlapping numbers mean? Look at the map on the next two pages, press your book wide open so that the map lays completely flat, and then follow the instructions from the poem. You'll be sure to find the code quickly.

Ryan closed his eyes for a moment and tried to collect his thoughts. "What do we do now?" he asked. "Do we give the treasure to Smith?"

"First, we have to *find* it," Sarah replied. "And yes, then I'll turn the coins over to them. So they'll leave me alone." She looked into Ryan's eyes. "Are you going to stop me?"

Ryan looked at her seriously. "Honestly, I have no idea what to do. And I don't really know what I would've done in your place. The only thing I know for sure is that we're pretty close to solving this whole thing. So we should keep going and try to find that solution."

Sarah took Ryan's hand and squeezed it. "Thank you for this."

He raised his eyebrows mockingly. "It's not like I have a choice. You know karate and judo – I only know sudoku."

Sarah had to laugh and, at least for the moment, the whole situation seemed a little less depressing.

They followed the route marked on the map until the tunnel widened and grew into a sort of natural cave, large enough to hold perhaps a dozen people. Empty oil lamps on the walls and the remains of old wooden benches suggested that this might have been some sort of underground communal room for the workers. On the far side, another tunnel extended into the darkness.

"This should be it," Sarah stated. "Do you see anything?"

They searched the area, which wasn't easy, because they didn't know what they were looking for: was it another letter? A treasure chest? Or something else entirely?

This time it was Sarah who found something: there was a strange pattern carved into the underside of one of the benches.

"This shape... it's a layout of this cave!" Sarah realized.

"And these numbers will probably tell us exactly where to find something here," Ryan added.

"Maybe even the treasure itself," Sarah guessed.

Ryan looked around. "It would certainly be a good place to hide it."

Ryan and Sarah are looking for a location in the cave, but you need the code to the page where the story continues. Take a close look at the illustration on the next page! Can you make sense of the jumble of numbers? If you follow the examples, you will be able to decipher the code.

"There it is!" Ryan pointed to a spot on the peninsula surrounded by a few stones. "That's the spot the riddle points to."

"Good work, Creed." Smith rubbed his hands together. "Hector, get to it!"

The burly bodyguard stepped forward, walked to the spot Ryan had found on the map, and plunged the shovel into the ground. As he did so, Smith grabbed Ryan's arm. He pulled out a jackknife and pressed it against Ryan's side.

"Just a precaution, Mr. Creed. So you don't get any funny ideas."

"That wasn't the deal," Ryan hissed.

"Neither was freeing your hands," Smith retorted.

Ryan looked at Sarah, who was no better off than he was; Gus had also drawn a knife and was holding her at bay.

The group watched in silence as Hector dug deeper and deeper. The sun was slowly setting behind the peaks and Ryan wondered how long it would be before it got dark.

The blade made him uneasy, and he decided it might be a good idea to engage Smith in conversation. An old tactic for dealing with hostage-takers: if you make them see you as human, it makes it harder for them to hurt or kill you.

"What are you going to do with the money when you find it, Smith?" asked Ryan.

"I told you, the less you know about me, the better for you."

"I'm not asking you to unravel your whole evil master plan for me like a movie villain. I'm just interested in the principle. If we find the coins, you'll have more money than you can ever spend, even if you sell them on the black market for far less than they're worth. What will you do with it? Will you settle down and become a respectable man? Surely you won't make another catch like *this.*"

Smith shook his head. "Do you really think I'm doing all this for the money? If I did, I could have quit a long time ago." He smiled. "What excites me is *power.* Money is just a means to an end. It's there to be spent. To be invested. Not to be hoarded." Smith raised an eyebrow. "Have you never harbored the desire to have power over others, Mr. Creed?"

"Absolutely not!" Ryan gasped. "Too much responsibility."

"Interesting," Smith muttered. "I'm sure a therapist would enjoy such a pronounced rejectionist attitude."

"The same probably applies to your striving for power," Ryan countered.

That answer was a bit risky – a test of sorts, Ryan thought. Smith's reaction might give him a clue as to whether he'd managed to establish a rapport with the guy.

He half-expected a kick to the hollow of his knee or a punch in the gut, but instead Smith just laughed approvingly. "Touché, Mr. Creed. Well played."

Ryan felt a small glimmer of hope. Perhaps he had managed to curry favor with Smith.

Moments later, they finally heard the shovel hitting something hard.

121

"What's that, Hector?" Smith called out.

"A safe, sir!" came the reply.

Ryan noticed that in spite of everything, his heart was beating faster, but with excitement instead of fear. Had they achieved their objective? Was this the treasure they had been after all this time?

They took a few steps closer to the hole Hector was just climbing out of. Sure enough, the top of a massive steel vault protruded from it. Ryan saw markings on it, but they were too dirty to make out.

Smith turned to Ryan. "Knowing our friend Reginald Dash, this vault likely holds yet another riddle. Hector is a capable man, but manual dexterity is not one of his strengths. I'd like you to take charge to make sure no important clues are destroyed."

Ryan looked at Smith questioningly. "You want me to keep digging? And what if I refuse?"

"Then I'll consider all aspects of our agreement null and void, Mr. Creed. Remember, I don't need you anymore. I already have what I want. Hector's little sawing toy would probably be pushed to its limits with a safe like this, but, if necessary, I could load the safe onto the helicopter and open it elsewhere. But that would mean unnecessary work and loss of time. If you cooperate with me now, you may escape with your life."

"*May?*" Ryan snapped in disgust. "We had a deal!"

Smith smiled. "I've learned two important things as a businessman. First, sometimes contracts need to be broken. And second, you should always have a plan B."

With that, Smith pulled out a small revolver he had hidden in his suit.

"You *asshole*!" Sarah blurted out.

"You didn't *really* think I only had one gun with me, did you? So come on Creed, dig. Unless the two of you would prefer to die right now!"

Hector shoved Ryan into the hole with the safe.

Thoughts raced through Ryan's mind as he picked up the shovel and pushed it into the dirt.

That worked out really well to establish a connection with the kidnapper, he thought sarcastically. *Typical Ryan Creed – always overestimating yourself!*

He inwardly told himself to get his act together. Blaming himself was useless now. The important thing was to analyze the situation.

If all the deals were off, there was no point in hoping Smith would let them go. They were now redundant – and this lake was an ideal place to dispose of them. Once this vault was opened, they would be as good as dead.

But if he refused to solve the puzzle, or if he failed, Smith would eventually lose patience too. So how were they going to get out of this mess?

He looked at Sarah. Maybe she had a plan to deal with this overpowering opponent? It didn't look like it. Smith was keeping her at arm's length with his gun drawn.

If she tried anything, he would have plenty of time to pull the trigger.

Maybe this was some kind of higher justice, Ryan thought. His thoughtlessness had inadvertently caused the death of Marcus's ex-girlfriend, and now it would kill him as well.

Back then, right after he left the FBI, he would have almost welcomed it. Not that he had ever thought about suicide, but a person had died as a result of his actions. He couldn't just shrug that off.

It had taken him a while to put his life back together. First, he had moved back home, as if he could undo everything that had happened since his school days.

His parents hadn't asked too many questions and welcomed him back into their home. In the end, strangely, it was their deaths that allowed Ryan to start over.

They had been killed in a traffic accident. Some jerk in a car that was way too big and way too heavy had crashed head-on into them. The coroner said they had died instantly.

The shock had jolted Ryan out of the stupor he had fallen into since his resignation. He had nothing and no one left to cling to. If he wanted his life to have any meaning, it was up to him to give it meaning.

And so the Foundation had been born. An attempt to right the wrongs of his past. A place where people would be taken seriously when they denounced violence or unjust police practices.

The Foundation was his legacy. And thanks to the generous check he had received from Power, it would live on even without Ryan.

In a way, the thought of Sarah's possible death moved him more than his own. For Sarah to die, Ryan thought, would seem utterly unfair. All Sarah had done was protect her daughter. And now she could die because it was the most convenient solution for this Smith. It was a damn disgrace, nothing less. Ryan was going to make sure it would not come to that, whatever it took.

That too would be a kind of higher justice, it occurred to him. Saving one life to atone for the loss of another.

He laughed bitterly. In theory, it was a wonderful idea. There was just one catch: he had no clue how to get Sarah or himself out of this situation.

Ryan couldn't work very fast, but he finally exposed the safe. He wiped the dirt off with his hand, revealing black markings on the door.

Below the combination lock, Reginald's son Stuart's name had been drawn in large, ornate letters. Above the lock was a pattern of black dots and dashes. Morse code. Ryan knew it like the back of his hand. This was it. Once this puzzle was solved, the safe would open!

Can you crack the combination to the safe?
Morse code is pretty simple, isn't it?

126

Two hours later, Ryan buckled his seat belt on the plane.

He had the window seat. Next to him, Sarah Corbet made herself as comfortable as possible in the aisle seat. Even though the tickets said "First Class" and the seats weren't quite as cramped as in Economy, this was still a short-haul domestic flight – you couldn't really expect luxury.

"Can I tell you something?" asked Sarah Corbet as the cabin door closed. "I didn't actually think you'd come. You seem rather... cautious."

"Let's put it this way: you and your boss have left a lot of tracks by now – you're hardly planning on doing me any harm. Shell companies and aliases provide no cover once the police have started an intensive investigation."

She smiled. "That may be a reason not to get too concerned, Mr. Creed, but it's not a good enough reason to come with me. Why didn't you just get in your car and go home?"

Ryan thought about it. Should he tell her the truth? A part of him resisted. Sarah Corbet was obviously withholding information, so it would make sense for him to do the same.

On the other hand, he remembered a bar conversation he had once had with an interrogation specialist. "The toughest guys," he had said, "are the ones who tell almost the whole truth. Those who keep quiet arouse suspicion, and those who tell a bunch of lies end up getting caught up in them. But if someone sticks almost completely to the truth, and only deviates from it in a few strategically important points – then it's hard as hell picking out those few lies from the mass of truth."

His motivation for coming along was no big secret, he finally decided, and he saw no reason to invent tall tales.

"I have a weakness," he answered truthfully. "I'm a curious guy. And your boss has gone to great lengths to exploit that weakness. What can I say? It worked. When someone begs so desperately to meet with me, there comes a point when I can no longer refuse."

Sarah's expression became serious. "That's a very dangerous philosophy in the long run. Sometimes it's important to put your own interests above those of others."

Ryan frowned. "Is that some kind of threat? Or are you telling me that I made the wrong choice when I got on this plane?"

She shook her head. "No. It was more of a general warning. You won't regret getting on this plane." She leaned back, plugged in a pair of earbuds, and closed her eyes.

A moment later, the roar of the engines swelled as the plane accelerated for takeoff.

I hope she's right, Ryan thought as the plane rose into the air and the airport below them grew smaller and smaller.

It was already late afternoon when they landed in Seattle. Since neither of them had checked any luggage, it was only a few minutes before they were walking across the airport parking lot to Sarah Corbet's car.

Ryan took a deep breath, savoring the cool ocean air – he really missed this climate in the Midwest. Then he noticed with surprise the vehicle they were heading towards.

"Quite a contrast to the car from this morning," he commented as Sarah opened the massive SUV that was easily three times the size of Ryan's own car.

"The limo was rented and had only one purpose: to impress you and show you that Will has money. It served that purpose." She gestured to the mountains on the horizon. "Look at this landscape. Do you think a luxury car would get me very far here?"

Ryan raised his eyebrows. "You rented it to *impress* me? You think money would have that effect on me?"

Sarah Corbet got into the car and opened the passenger door for him. "It has that effect on everyone, Mr. Creed. *Everyone* is impressed by money."

On the way into town, Ryan glanced at his watch. "Can we stop at a store before you take me to the hotel? I don't have anything with me."

"We're not going to the hotel. Will wants to talk to you immediately."

"Today?! It's almost six o'clock!"

"Will usually stays in the office until ten. And he's made it very clear that he wants to talk to you right away."

"Oh. And I'm guessing I have no say in the matter, do I?"

"Not in this case, Mr. Creed. Will is not someone to be kept waiting."

129

Sarah Corbet knew her way around Seattle well. She used back roads and side streets to avoid the worst of the traffic, and they arrived at their destination much earlier than Ryan had expected.

It was a high-rise office building in the South Lake Union district, one of the most expensive business locations in the city. It was the kind of neighborhood where global corporations had their headquarters, but there was no company logo anywhere on the building into whose underground garage Sarah was now driving. As far as Ryan could tell, it was an anonymous structure of glass and steel.

The parking lot was virtually empty – and very clean. Colored lines on the walls marked parking zones and pointed the way to the exits. There was no sign of the typical soot buildup caused by exhaust fumes. Ryan wondered if this was an indication that the building was new or recently renovated, or if it meant that most of the employees drove electric cars. Maybe a combination of both.

They got out and Sarah Corbet headed for a heavy fire door. Ryan didn't follow. "What are you waiting for?" she asked after a few steps, turning around.

"Explanations," Ryan said. "I'm not moving another foot until someone tells me what the *hell* is going on."

"And you chose *this* place to find out? The middle of an underground garage?"

"The more unpleasant the environment, the greater the general interest in getting out of it quickly. In other words, I'm more likely to get answers here than in some penthouse or corner office."

Sarah sighed. "All right, Mr. Creed. What do you want me to explain?"

Ryan shook his head. "Not you. I want to talk to this ominous 'Will Power.' You said he was in his office. Then he's more than welcome to come down here."

She raised her eyebrows. "Mr. Power is an extremely busy man. You really can't expect him to drop everything to make his way to an underground garage."

"Your Mr. Power spent a lot of money to get *me* to drop everything and fly out here. If it's so important to him, surely he can take the elevator down a few floors. Alternatively, you can give him my best regards while I call a cab back to the airport."

She frowned, moved far enough away from Ryan so he couldn't overhear, then pulled out her cell phone. Sarah Corbet's face and posture looked tense during the call, Ryan observed.

After a few sentences, she hung up before rejoining him.

"He's on his way," she explained curtly. "I do hope you didn't piss him off with that."

"I'll take my chances," came Ryan's cool reply.

Continue reading on page 077.

"Ryan! Are you daydreaming again?" Sarah's voice over the helicopter's headset brought him back to the present.

They were approaching the mountain range, and Sarah's attention was focused on avoiding flying too close to the treetops. "Sorry, I was thinking," Ryan apologized. "What's up?"

"According to the satellite image, the Kern & Miller mine should be in a clearing," she explained to Ryan. "There are also some old buildings there. Let me know if you see anything!"

Ryan squinted and watched the coniferous forest pass below them. Birds fluttered away, startled by the noise of the helicopter.

There! In the distance, he spotted a bright patch in the middle of the dark green forest. He pointed it out to Sarah.

"That could be it," she said, setting course for the spot Ryan had indicated.

He had been right. The bright patch turned out to be a fairly large clearing. From above, Ryan could make out two ramshackle-looking barracks, their wood ash-gray from weathering, and the pitiful remains of other buildings that must have collapsed long ago.

Sarah maneuvered the helicopter to a point where it was a good distance from any obstacles and touched down smoothly.

"Wait for the rotor to stop before you get out," she said, "it's safer that way."

132

The sound of the engine died away and a strange silence surrounded them: no cars or buses, no air conditioners or beeping traffic lights, just the sound of the wind in the branches and the chirping of the birds, which tentatively resumed after the helicopter had gone silent.

Ryan got out and breathed in the forest air. He could not remember the last time he had been so far out in nature. It was noticeably cooler up here than in the city, but it wasn't an unpleasant chill; it was refreshing, like plunging into the water of a clear mountain lake.

Sarah pointed to one of the two wooden buildings that was still reasonably intact. "Look over there. That looks like it could have been the company store. Don't you think?"

Ryan agreed. There was a faded sign above the door, the writing no longer visible, and through the empty window openings, he could see some shelves inside.

As they entered, Ryan was surprised at how well preserved everything was. Sure, the elements had taken their toll over time: the wooden furniture smelled moldy, and there were several places where the roof had caved in, burying parts of the furniture. But there were no signs of vandalism. The mine was probably too remote for that. Where the roof had held, everything seemed to be exactly as it had been when the mine had been abandoned nearly a hundred years ago.

The company store appeared to be modeled after the general stores of the day, with a large sales counter separating customers from the shelves of merchandise. On it sat an old-fashioned cash register, its ornate housing completely encrusted with rust.

Something round and metallic glittered on the floor. Ryan picked it up, wiped off the dust, and examined it: it was a coin, similar to the one they had found earlier. Company scrip from the Kern & Miller mine.

"Looks like we're in the right place," he said.

Sarah nodded. "And I guess if Reginald Dash gave us a coin as a clue, then it's pretty clear where we should be looking."

The surface of the register was rough with rust, and no matter how much they rattled and tugged, it was impossible to open.

"Maybe we need to enter a code with the keys?" Sarah wondered.

"Impossible," Ryan replied. "They're so corroded, we'd never be able to do that. Besides, we don't have a code."

"Then I guess we'll have to use force again."

Ryan hated to see Sarah pick up the old cash register and smash it on the floor. It was an antique and deserved to be treated with more respect!

Sarah remained pragmatic: "You can find old cash registers like this in any junk shop. And in much better condition. We're interested in what's inside – *that's* unique."

"There aren't any coins in there, though," he said. "We would have heard them when you picked it up."

"So what – it might not be a coin, but it's the next clue!"

Sarah breathed heavily as she picked up the register and slammed it down on the ground once more.

This time something happened: with a *bang*, the drawer popped out!

Crouching down, Ryan inspected the register.

"Empty," he announced disappointedly. But then he had an idea. "Maybe it's not *in* the drawer at all...."

He slid his hand into the drawer and felt the metal of the cash register's casing. There was something there! An envelope was stuck above the drawer, under the cash register mechanism.

Ryan carefully dislodged it and pulled it out. It still looked brand-new, as if it had just been put there. It had clearly been well protected from light and moisture by the casing.

Ryan opened the envelope and pulled out a piece of paper. It was so thin it was almost see-through, and there was a maze-like pattern of lines and symbols on both sides.

"Looks like a map," Sarah guessed. "Probably of the mine."

Start
B
A
C

Finish

Ryan looked at the paper more closely. "But I don't really understand the map. Maybe it'll make more sense once we find the entrance to the mine."

Sarah nodded, and they headed for the store's exit.

The mine entrance wasn't hard to find; it was just past the remains of the old workers' dwellings.

The mine itself was anything but inviting: a gloomy tunnel bathed in total darkness. Cool air emanated from inside, and there was the lazy sound of dripping water.

"Is it still safe?" asked Ryan.

Sarah hesitated, then looked at him. "Maybe you're right. I think I'd better go in alone."

"Excuse me? How are you going to do this without me?"

"You won't believe this, but I'm doing very well in life without a man's omnipresent guidance."

"That's not what I mean! What about the map – we have no idea how to read it, and Power hired me to figure out this exact kind of thing. If I don't, there'll be no money for the Foundation!"

Sarah fiddled nervously with her flashlight. "It's not like we have to tell him."

Ryan raised his hand. "Wait a minute – what's going on? You make it sound like you don't *want* me to come!"

Sarah sighed, then turned away. "Fine, you win. Come with me!"

"Wait, you can't just..."

But Sarah could; ignoring Ryan's calls, she just kept walking.

He had no choice but to follow her into the mine. The light from Sarah's flashlight fell on the heavy wooden beams that supported the tunnel. The ground was rough and pebbly at first, but after a few steps it became smoother. They passed stacks of wood and small piles of coal left behind by the mine's last users.

Once more Ryan tried to question Sarah's behavior, but she just ignored him and walked deeper into the mine. Following her, Ryan glanced back and saw the entrance behind them getting smaller and smaller.

After about twenty yards, the passage took a sharp turn, and the last remnants of daylight faded. In the glare of the flashlight, they saw some kind of wooden scaffolding, and behind it, something long and metallic glittered on the floor. Sarah was the first to realize what it was: "Rails! And a buffer stop! It must be a mine train."

"There's something on the map that looks like mine carts," Ryan confirmed. He glanced at the paper to determine their location. There wasn't anything that looked like a buffer stop on either side.

They continued cautiously until they came to an intersection. From here, three passages led deeper into the mountain. Which would be the right one?

"At least we know where we are now," Ryan explained, pointing to a spot on the map where this intersection was clearly visible. "But how do we figure out where to go?"

He looked at the symbols again. "These could be coal piles. And there! Look!"

He pointed to some rubble just to the right of the path. "I think that's marked right here!"

Sarah understood. "This stuff isn't lying around here by accident!"

Ryan nodded. "But we're still missing something. Is there anything in the book that might help us?"

Sarah took out the notebook and flipped through it. Then she laughed triumphantly. "Yes, this must be it!"

Ryan studied the page while flipping the map back and forth. "All right!" he declared. "I think I got it."

What did Ryan discover? Why don't you cut out the map from pages 135 and 136 so you can work on the puzzle too? The answer must be connected to the routes through the tunnels. Pay close attention to the piles of coal, the rubble, and the wooden planks. And what about the wagons? It looks like each one has its own tunnel entrance and exit. Trace the right paths carefully and you're sure to see the light soon!

When Ryan arrived at the college the next morning, he was met in the hallway by Travis Martin. Travis was in charge of the schedules and one of the nicest people Ryan knew. Whenever his short, stocky frame showed up anywhere, it was like a good buddy approaching.

So Ryan was all the more surprised when Travis put a hand on his arm and said sternly, "Would you step into my office for a minute? We need to talk."

Ryan had never known Travis to want to discuss *anything* in his office. He usually settled things over a cup of coffee in the staff room.

Travis was a fast walker. Too fast to start a conversation with him on the way to the office. Ryan wondered what could have happened. Had someone died? Maybe someone complained about him? He wasn't aware of any wrongdoing on his part, but that didn't necessarily mean anything.

It was immediately apparent that Travis rarely used his office for meetings. Books, files, and papers littered every available surface, and Travis had to clear a pile of junk off a chair before Ryan could sit down.

"So come on, spill it," Ryan demanded. "What happened?"

"I was actually hoping you could explain that to me, Ryan. Why didn't you tell me before?"

"What are you *talking* about? *What* was I supposed to tell you?"

Travis sighed. "Come on, surely you understand that I need a little planning security.

"Dropping something like this on me out of the blue is *not* very polite."

"I honestly have no idea what you're talking about," Ryan insisted.

Travis looked at Ryan in surprise. "You don't know *anything* about this?" he exclaimed. "But that makes no sense at all!"

"Neither does the way you keep saying 'this' without just telling me what 'this' is. Can you please just *explain* to me what's going on?"

"Last night I got a call from the dean's office: you're excused from teaching, effective immediately."

Ryan's jaw dropped. "What, they're kicking me out?"

"On the contrary. You're excused for the next ten days on full pay. Practically a paid vacation, except you don't even have to take any vacation days."

"The dean's office *gives* me ten days off just like that? Why?"

"That's exactly what *I* asked. At first, they wouldn't give me a straight answer. Eventually they let it slip that someone else had given them something, too."

Ryan looked at Travis in confusion.

"A donation, Ryan. Someone gave them a bunch of money on the condition that you don't teach for a little while."

"Who would *do* that?" Ryan asked, leaning forward and accidentally knocking over a stack of papers on Travis's desk. The papers slid off and landed in a messy pile on the floor.

"*Oops.* Sorry about that."

Ryan started to pick up the papers, but Travis stopped him. "Don't worry, I'll take care of it. You better go and enjoy your days off."

Ryan stood up. "And what if I don't want to take them?"

"Not a chance. The schedule has been rearranged. Melissa's covering most of your classes, Ben's taking the rest." Travis lowered his voice. "The dean's office has made it *very* clear to me that they don't want to see you teaching for the next ten days. Must be a hell of a lot of money. You can see why I assumed you knew about it. I thought you might have some influential acquaintances from your past who still owe you a favor."

Ryan shook his head. "Believe me, I don't know anybody like that. I don't want to *meet* anybody like that either."

He started for the door and then stopped. "Tell me, Travis, is there any chance that this money came from the Seattle area?"

At a loss, Travis shrugged. "I don't know, nobody told me."

"I'm sorry, but I'm not allowed to disclose financial information, Mr. Creed." Mike from the secretary's office was usually very eager to help and make life easier for the staff, but this time Ryan was getting nowhere with him. "We have a very strict confidentiality policy. If I don't adhere to it, I'll be out of a job in no time."

It was clear to see that Mike was genuinely sorry. Frowning under his blond mane of curls, he had a look on his face that reminded Ryan of a disappointed puppy.

"I don't want you to mention any amounts," Ryan tried again. "Or even the sender, or the bank. I know this transfer was received here. All I'm interested in is the location of the financial institution that sent it."

Mike thought for a moment. "No, I'm afraid that's really not possible," he explained slowly. "I'm not at liberty to discuss the matter. Even if – purely hypothetically speaking – even *if* it had been an unusual place and I had noticed it – say, because it wasn't in the U.S. but some offshore location – even *then* I wouldn't be allowed to tell you. I'm really sorry I can't help you with this."

Ryan suppressed a grin. He knew that he could rely on Mike. "Thank you, I understand. I'm sorry to have bothered you."

"No problem! And please forgive me for not being able to tell you anything."

"It's all forgiven, Mike. All forgiven."

So it was an offshore account. That made sense. This weird "Tickets for Ryan Creed, Inc." was also based in the Bahamas.

But what was the point of all this hide-and-seek? Whoever was behind it must have known that it didn't exactly inspire confidence. After all, who would agree to take a flight into the unknown at the expense of a complete stranger?

He stepped into the parking lot to go to his car. At that moment, a dark sedan, which had been lurking in the shadows a short distance away, began to approach.

It wasn't one of those stretch limos that teenagers rented for prom, but it was still unusually large and luxurious for this neighborhood, and especially for a college parking lot.

It didn't take much deductive reasoning to suspect a connection between this vehicle and Ryan's anonymous benefactor.

Sure enough, the car pulled up right next to him. The door opened and the driver got out: a tall young woman with sleek black hair and warm brown skin, wearing a business suit that looked both elegant and comfortable at the same time. Everything fit her so perfectly that Ryan suspected it was tailor-made.

"Mr. Creed," the woman said. It wasn't a question; it was a statement. She knew it was him.

Ryan studied her cautiously. "And you are...?"

"Sarah Corbet. Good morning!"

She came toward him and held out her hand, but Ryan didn't take it.

"Why did you arrange all this?" Ryan demanded. "The letter, the plane ticket, the donation..."

She lowered her outstretched arm. "You really are as quick on the draw as they say."

"What did you do all this for?" Ryan repeated.

Sarah Corbet shook her head. "It wasn't me; it was my employer."

Ryan smiled. "Ah, the mysterious benefactor."

"He's not so mysterious. He wants to meet you. That's why all the fuss."

"In Seattle, I guess?"

She nodded.

"Then why didn't he just *call* me?"

Sarah Corbet's face flashed a brief smile.

"He likes to do things his way. You'll understand better when you get to know him."

"*If* I get to know him,'" Ryan corrected her.

She pulled an envelope from the inside pocket of her top. "Here's your ticket. Flight leaves in two hours."

"I haven't said 'yes' yet," Ryan pointed out. "And I don't intend to."

She shrugged. "Will warned me you might say something like that."

"Will?" Ryan asked.

"My boss. Will Power."

Ryan laughed. "*Will Power*?!" he repeated incredulously. "You're not serious, are you? That's by far the stupidest alias I've ever heard!"

She was unmoved. "He may not have picked a very original one, but it describes his character very accurately."

"And what did he instruct you to do in case I didn't want to accompany you? Will you kidnap me?"

Sarah Corbet shook her head. "No. If you wish, I will leave and no one will ever bother you again. I was merely told to inform you that you would be throwing away the chance to solve a riddle greater than anything you have ever encountered. And that you would never find out exactly what it was about."

She looked at her watch, then at him. "You have exactly five minutes to decide."

Continue reading on page 126.

"What are you *waiting* for?" the voice repeated. "Put your hands in the air and turn around!"

Slowly, Ryan and Sarah stood, obeying the order.

In front of them were two men. Both had guns. Ryan figured that one of them was a classic "heavy" – a goon, in underworld slang. Goons were usually built like tanks, all brawn and no brains. He was wearing an ill-fitting suit, and the contrast between his clothes and his physique oddly added to his intimidation factor.

The man next to him was the complete opposite: slim and tall and with the smooth swagger of a dancer. He looked as if he had stepped straight from a dinner party into the coal mine.

"Mr. Smith, I presume?" said Ryan to the slim one.

"Correct," he replied without lowering his gun. "I've heard a lot about you, Mr. Creed, and I'm delighted to finally make your acquaintance."

Ryan looked down the barrel and tried his best to hide his nervousness from Smith. He didn't like guns. He never had. "I'm afraid I can't say the pleasure is all mine at the moment," he replied with forced coolness. "I'm not sure if that's because you're waving a gun in my face or because you're threatening Sarah Corbet's child. Both, I think."

"A good businessman always covers his back, Mr. Creed. I'm sure that doesn't surprise you, does it?"

He turned to Sarah. "So I'd like to ask you to hand over Dash's notes to me now. From now on, *I'm* in charge."

Looking at the guns pointed at her, Sarah resigned herself and pulled out Reginald Dash's journal.

"Why did you follow us here?" she asked as she handed the book to the gangster. "I intended to bring you the coins anyway!"

"Trust is good, but control is better," Smith replied coldly as he leafed through the notebook with a satisfied expression. "You obviously had no problem deceiving your employer. How could I be sure you wouldn't pull the same trick on *me*?" Smith smiled through gleaming white teeth. "I suggest we bring this matter to a close. You found everything, I presume?"

"We found what's *here*," Ryan corrected him. "But we haven't assessed it yet."

"No problem," Smith explained. "I quite enjoy inspecting the goods myself." He turned to the burly bodyguard. "Hector, would you mind taking a look?"

Ryan glanced at the cage construction holding the box, and a suspicion grew in him. He stepped aside. Out of the corner of his eye, he checked that the metal plate with the warning was positioned so that the text on it was not visible.

Hector knelt by the hole, and indeed, he ignored the metal plate. Instead, he scraped at the cage bars and the box with his clawlike hands. He tugged and shook at it, but it wouldn't budge.

149

With a huff, he pulled a small circular saw from an inside pocket.

"This guy has a *power saw* on him?" Ryan blurted out. "Who carries *that* kind of hardware?"

Smith smiled weakly and pointed to Ryan's lumberjack shirt. "I could ask the same question about your fashionable outfit. The answer would be the same in both cases: people who want to be prepared. There's always a chance you might have to *chop something up* unexpectedly." He looked Ryan up and down ominously.

Hector started the power saw, and a moment later, the teeth of the saw were digging into the metal, screeching and sparking. Ryan wanted to cover his ears, but he didn't dare move.

The tool did a good job, cutting through the metal bar in less than a minute.

Ryan watched as Hector started the next cut.

"I hope you know what you're doing," he said to Smith.

"Oh, I know very well. I'm going to get what's rightfully mine." The sound of the circular saw interrupted the conversation for a moment.

"What do you mean?" asked Sarah when it was quiet again. "Are you related to Dash?"

"You don't want to know too much about me. At least, not if you have any hope of getting out of here alive." Smith thought for a moment. "But, to satisfy your curiosity, no, I have no connection to Reginald Dash. But I have a score to settle with your Mr. Power. His activities have disrupted my affairs, so I think it's only legitimate for me to pay him back in kind."

Another shrill scream from the circular saw echoed around the cave.

Ryan could easily imagine what kind of affairs might have been involved.

This Smith looked like a Mafia cliché in the flesh. He didn't know exactly what had happened between him and Power, but he guessed that it had probably involved gold laundering. He was familiar with cases like this from his time with the FBI. Smith had found a niche where he could turn his illegal earnings into seemingly legal profits – questionable real estate deals? Shady casinos? But then Power had stepped in and used his capital to corner the market. Or at least brought so much attention to it that Smith no longer felt comfortable there. And depending on how badly things had gone for Smith, it was quite possible that he had lost a lot of money.

Ryan knew people who had committed murder for such things. Smith, on the other hand, was determined to get his hands on the rare Double Eagle coins, probably worth many times what he had lost.

Finally, the circular saw fell silent and Ryan looked at the cage. There were now large gaps in two of the bars, big enough to pull out the box. But it also seemed to Ryan that the shape of the cage had changed somewhat. He thought back to the warning on the metal plate, and his earlier suspicion was confirmed.

"Very well done, Hector," Smith praised. "Now bring the item to me, please."

"Watch out!" Ryan whispered to Sarah as Smith spoke. "Something's about to happen."

Hector reached into the cage and grabbed the exposed sides of the box with his hands. He tensed his muscles and pulled so hard that it made the veins in his temples stand out.

Ryan watched him anxiously. He didn't know exactly what would happen if the box was moved. But he was sure that *something* would happen. And he hoped it would give Sarah and him an advantage.

With a triumphant scream, Hector pulled the box from its hole in the ground.

"How heavy is it?" Smith wanted to know.

"Very light," Hector replied. "Too light for gold coins, if you ask me."

"Damn! Is there no end to this scavenger hunt?"

Smith had barely finished his sentence when all hell broke loose.

Over the past few minutes, Ryan had realized that what had enclosed the metal box wasn't just a cage. Reginald Dash had chosen the hiding place with great care. The steel structure that Ryan and Sarah had uncovered had been placed by Dash to support the pillar above it and was itself reinforced from the inside by the metal box.

The installation of this construction must have been quite complex and risky, Ryan guessed, but somehow Dash had managed it.

The purpose of the structure became clear the moment Hector had pulled the box from the ground. The metal cage had already been weakened by the sawing of the bars. Now, stripped of the structural support of the box inside, it could no longer withstand the weight of the pillar. But this was only the first domino in a chain reaction. With a *crunch*, the wooden support buckled, cracked, and shattered. All Hector could do to get to safety was jump to the side as a load of earth collapsed directly onto the ground where he had been digging. This collapse in turn increased the load on the next pair of pillars in the tunnel. They swayed, then buckled, disappearing under an avalanche of debris and earth, blocking the way back.

Everyone had recoiled in shock, and it took them a moment to make sense of the dull roar that continued for seconds after the collapse, then slowly faded.

"That didn't only happen here," Ryan said, as the reality of the situation dawned on him. "Half the entire mine has collapsed."

Continue reading on page 014.

For a moment, Ryan stared at the solution, perplexed. Three numbers: 6, 4, and 3. Nothing else. No marketing slogan, no link to a website with more information. Just three numbers. What could it mean?

There was no question in his mind that there *was* a meaning. No one would go to all that trouble just to send him three meaningless numbers!

"Not quite as simple as expected," he muttered approvingly.

Once more, Ryan scrutinized the sheet of paper. He checked its thickness to see if it could be separated into two thinner layers, felt for irregularities in the surface that might indicate invisible ink, and held it up to the light. But to no avail. It seemed as if the letter had given up all its secrets.

Ryan smiled. The letter had no more secrets, perhaps – but not necessarily the *envelope*!

He picked up the empty envelope and examined it, just as he had the letter. He immediately noticed the quality of the paper: it was thick and beautifully finished, as he had come to expect from very old books. When Ryan held the envelope up to the light of his floor lamp, he realized why: in the upper right corner, just below the stamp, letters and numbers shimmered through:

CREED PNR VCP47 _ _ _

A watermark with his name! *That* was an extraordinary amount of effort for a promotional puzzle.

This kind of thing could only be added at the paper manufacturing stage. This meant that this envelope had been made especially for him! Who would have gone to so much trouble to deliver such a message?

Ryan made a note of the character sequence and took a closer look. The first thing he noticed were the three blanks at the end. The obvious next step was to insert the three numbers from the puzzle:

CREED PNR VCP47 643

"Creed" was his last name – that wasn't much of a challenge. But the rest? The last sequence of characters looked a bit like the car license plates Ryan had seen on British TV shows. But he couldn't imagine that he was supposed to track down a car owner in the UK to solve the mystery.

Those three letters in the middle, "PNR" – if he could figure out what they meant, he would certainly be a big step closer. Maybe it was an abbreviation? He picked up one of his encyclopedias – volume 20: *Pluto to Quebec.*

He rejected most explanations for PNR. Ryan didn't believe it was a reference to the Cuban *Policía Nacional Revolucionaria*, and it probably didn't mean political parties in Portugal or Romania any more than it meant the international code for a railway station.

He thought something else was far more likely: *a passenger name record, a data set that contains all the important details of a booked airline ticket and is usually assigned an alphanumeric code.*

An alphanumeric code – that description certainly fit "VCP47 643" pretty well. And with that, he knew what to do next.

Ryan picked up his phone.

"Ryan! To what do I owe this honor?" Craig sounded genuinely pleased.

It was getting harder and harder for travel agencies to find customers these days. A regular customer like Ryan, who consistently refused to book online, was worth their weight in gold. "Time for another trip to the coast? Or is there a new puzzle championship?"

"No, not this time. I just wanted to know something. If I give you the number of a passenger name record, can you find out more about the reservation?"

"That depends. Not from the number alone, but if you also have the last name of the person traveling, it's no problem."

Ryan looked down at his notes. The name had been in the watermark: "Creed."

"This may sound stupid, Craig, but I think it's booked under my name."

"Are you being disloyal to me?" Ryan wasn't quite sure how much of the disappointment in Craig's voice was real and how much was feigned.

"Of course not. It's a long story, but I didn't book it myself."

"OK, let's hear it." Craig sounded skeptical but didn't ask any further questions.

Ryan gave him the code he had found. He could hear Craig typing before coming back with an answer a few seconds later.

"And you really didn't know about this ticket?"

"Not until a few minutes ago. Why?" asked Ryan.

"Because it's for tomorrow. A flight from here to Seattle. First class. With a hotel reservation."

Ryan sighed. Who on earth was booking flights and hotels for him behind his back?

"Does the PNR tell you anything about the buyer?" Ryan probed.

"Hang on. It was booked through one of those online platforms. Want to bet they didn't get as good a deal as I could? Looks like the buyer was a company..." Craig hesitated and then started to laugh. "You probably won't believe me, but the buyer's company name is Tickets for Ryan Creed, Inc."

Ryan was incredulous; someone had actually started his own company to hide behind *just* for this stuff! Craig didn't seem to have much to do that afternoon, and he also seemed to have become curious himself. Whatever the case, he was quick to offer his services to find out more about this ominous company, though not without a little ribbing about Ryan's internet abstinence. "If you were really serious about your refusal to use technology, you would fight me tooth and nail to keep me from looking into this for you."

"On the contrary," Ryan countered with a grin. "There are two ways to thwart effective surveillance. Either you make yourself as invisible as possible by leaving virtually no data trail, or you hide the really important information among so much junk data that it's practically impossible to filter out. So when you search on my behalf, you're protecting your own data at the same time."

"Are you *sure* you're not a lawyer?" Craig muttered.

Within a few minutes, Craig had pulled together all the information that could be found; apart from an entry in the commercial register, there was virtually nothing online about the company. The sole owner was a shell company in the Bahamas, but the owner of that company remained a mystery.

Next, Ryan asked Craig to look into events in Seattle. Maybe there was some kind of puzzle contest or something that someone was trying to bait him with. But nothing seemed to fit the bill.

"Right," Craig concluded, "do you want me to give you the ticket details?"

Ryan declined. "I don't like dancing to the tune of some anonymous whistle. The whole thing feels a little too much like stalking. Besides, I have work to do."

"Whatever you say." Craig took a more intimate tone now. "But just between us, you're curious, aren't you?"

Of *course* Ryan was curious. If he wasn't curious, he would never have come up with the idea of hacking into other people's servers when he was thirteen years old.

If he wasn't curious, he wouldn't spend hours and hours on increasingly difficult puzzles. And yes, there was that inner voice telling him to just get on that plane tomorrow and see what would happen.

But he had found that sometimes it was better not to listen to that voice. It was safer for him and for others.

So he waved it off. "Curiosity kills the cat, Craig. And I am quite fond of my life."

And that was the end of it for him. Well, almost. Sure, that inner voice hadn't gone completely silent, but as Ryan warmed up his dinner, he humored it with the prospect of spending the next few days investigating who was behind the ominous company Tickets for Ryan Creed, Inc.

And when the voice wouldn't shut up, even as he lay in bed, he tried to convince it – and himself – that he wasn't really trying to avoid the puzzle.

This isn't the end, he told himself. *It's the beginning. There are a thousand other ways to find out who is behind this letter. And all of them are safer than getting on that plane.*

Ryan also knew that those options were all more complicated and much less likely to succeed. But he preferred not to think about that for too long.

Continue reading on page 140.

<E-RazOr> Shall I start the script now?

Ryan's heart was pounding as he typed the message into the chat, and he glanced furtively at his bedroom door, which still had the dog poster Dad had put up for his eighth birthday. Ryan had locked himself in, but if Mom or Dad came home and knocked, he would have to open the door. And he didn't want them to know what he was doing.

<Doom98> NOT YET!!!!
<Doom98> Double-check everything first!
<Doom98> Is the VPN enabled? Is the proxy running and are you connected through the Tor router?

Just a year ago, Ryan had no idea what any of these terms meant. Back then, he was just looking for a way to get around the annoying parental control filter his mom had installed on the router at home. In the process, he discovered that there was a lot more interesting information out there than he could have hoped for.

It had been easy to override the filter, but after that, he had continued to read and learn, hanging out in the chat channels of the scene until he had earned some respect there. He enjoyed it. Ryan had just celebrated his twelfth birthday, and yet he already had the respect of people at least twice his age. Although they probably had no idea quite how young he was.

Sure, in the eyes of the regular users he was still a beginner, a "noob," but now they seemed to see talent in him – and at some point, one of them had agreed to show him a few more tricks.

<E-RazOr> All good.
<Doom98> OK!
<Doom98> Again, don't do anything stupid on the server.
<Doom98> Have a look around, but don't do any damage, and don't even think about data sharing!
<Doom98> Or you'll have the FBI knocking on your door before you know it!

Ryan hadn't even considered doing anything with the data. But now that Doom98 had so explicitly told him not to, he just had to ask.

<E-RazOr> If you're not doing anything, why are you hacking?
<Doom98> You'll find out in a minute....
<Doom98> Run the script.

The script in question was written by Ryan himself. With help from Doom98, of course. The fact that he did it himself was important. Hackers had always looked down on amateurs whose talents were limited to using scripted attack and cracking programs. They were contemptuously called "script kiddies": dumb kids who knew no better than to run other people's scripts. To be accepted, you had to understand what the program did and why it worked. Better yet, write it yourself. This one wasn't particularly complicated.

It could be used on a login form to automatically try various standard methods to gain access.

There were thousands of sites where you could download this kind of tool. But this one wasn't just downloaded from somewhere. It was Ryan's own brainchild. And now he was about to see it in action for the first time.

He had chosen an easy target. A small web shop that sold T-shirts and sneakers. Doom98 was right: it wasn't about what you found there, it was about the discovery itself, about accessing areas you weren't supposed to be in. It was about outsmarting the machine.

Ryan opened a terminal window and typed a command:

```
E-RazOr:~$ ./exscrpt.sh
```

For a moment, it seemed as if nothing was happening. Of course, Ryan knew that behind the scenes his script was gradually trying out every single attack he had programmed it with. But outwardly, there was nothing.

Ryan cursed silently and wished he had built some status messages into the program. Something that would tell him what it was doing. But all he could do was wait.

<E-RazOr> Could it be hanging?
<Doom98> Patience, kid. Patience.

Ryan was about to give up when, finally, something happened:

Operation complete. Output file written to disk.
<E-RazOr> It worked!

Holding his breath, Ryan opened the text file the script had generated. When he saw the information it contained, his heart skipped a beat: it was the store's entire user database! Complete with email addresses and passwords!

Ryan shook his head. Storing passwords in plain text was about the dumbest thing a developer could do. On the other hand, it did make his life easier.

He picked a random user and tried their credentials to log into the system.

It worked! He could see the address and past purchases of a woman from Minneapolis!

A sense of power washed over him. The information in front of him was information that was supposed to be off-limits to him. OK, so in this case, it was little more than just trivial information, but if it took this little effort to get a store's customer data, what secrets could he reveal if he really put his mind to it?

<E-RazOr> You're right! This is the bomb!

Continue reading on page 068.

Ryan returned the sheet to Power and told him the solution: "Three numbers: 6, 3, and 5. But without the map mentioned in the letter, it's probably of little use to you."

Power didn't answer right away. He looked down at his phone and then at Sarah Corbet. "Solved correctly. And in a very good time. I think it was worth it for you to bring him here."

"You already knew the solution!" Ryan gasped. "Then why are you paying me so much money for it?"

"I had to make sure that you were as good as your reputation. I hope you'll forgive me for this little test." Power took out his pen again, signed the check and handed it to Ryan. "Here you go, as promised."

Ryan hesitated. "Wait, I have a few questions first. And please be honest. If you lie to me, I'll find out sooner or later."

Power smiled. "On my word of honor, I'll answer your questions truthfully."

"Good. Is this blood money? Are you involved in any illegal activities?"

Sarah laughed. "Do you think Will is a drug lord or something?"

"I don't think anything. All I see is someone with a lot of money and I don't know where it came from. I don't want to accept gifts that people have suffered or died for."

Power gestured reassuringly and looked Ryan straight in the eye. "I give you my word of honor: I earned every cent I own completely legally."

"In what industry?"

"Information technology, Mr. Creed. I was lucky enough to be in the right place at the right time with the right talent. That's how I became one of the first employees of a garage company. They didn't have much money for a salary in those days, so they made me a partner instead. When I started, my shares were worth so little that the banks wouldn't accept them as collateral for a loan. But these days..." He gestured with his arm. "Let's put it this way: this building is not the only tower block I own. Not by a long shot."

Ryan knew that kind of biography. The gold-rush winners of the tech boom. As with any gold rush, they were the great exception to the rule. For every person who had amassed incredible wealth during this period, there were thousands who had narrowly missed the big time and were now living the lives of overworked employees – always with an eye on the chosen few who had done better than they had.

This "Will Power" had obviously been one of the lucky ones. That sounded plausible enough to Ryan. Then there was the very subjective impression that he just didn't *seem* like a criminal. Sure, Power had no problem flaunting his wealth, but not in the aggressively intimidating way Ryan had seen from people in the organized crime world.

A don wielded his power like a gun to your head. Will Power presented it as casually as an expensive watch on his wrist.

"OK, agreed." Ryan took the check. He looked at the signature. It didn't say "Will Power," but what it did say was impossible to decipher.

Will looked at Sarah Corbet. "I think you have some errands to run, don't you? Now would be a good time. I'll see you later."

Corbet nodded and got into the car.

Power turned to Ryan: "Would you mind if we went to my office, Mr. Creed? This isn't the most comfortable location for a long meeting."

Ryan nodded. It had been the right decision to have Power come down here, but there was no reason to stand around in the bleak parking garage any longer.

The elevator looked like every other office elevator Ryan had seen. It was polished and mirrored, but fortunately without that annoying music being played. Power pulled out a key and inserted it into a lock next to the top button. The doors closed.

"Next question," Ryan explained as the booth made its way up. "Why me? Why did you choose *me* specifically for your assignment?"

"Because you are the ideal choice. As you've already seen, there's been one puzzle, so I have reason to believe there will be more. You are a proven expert in puzzles, cryptology, and computer forensics. Although I don't think computers will play a major role here."

"Lucky for you. I'm no longer up to speed in that department."

"I know – which is odd, to be honest. You were well on your way to becoming the authority on computer crime. Hardly anyone knows what they want to do with themselves at that age, let alone have acquired the experience to walk straight into a well-paying position."

"It wasn't all *that* well-paying," Ryan said.

Power smiled. "Still. Why give up such a promising career?"

The way he asked the question, as if his wealth meant that he deserved to know anything about anyone, annoyed Ryan. Frankly, it made him *mad* as hell. Ryan's choices were his own, and he'd never felt the need to explain those choices to others. Not to the other faculty members, not to the students, and certainly not to this guy who called himself "Will Power."

He was silent for a moment before answering Power. "I had my reasons," Ryan explained succinctly.

The expression on the face of his enigmatic host remained impenetrable.

A *ping* announced that the elevator had reached its destination. The doors opened to reveal a spacious office with modern, sleek metal and dark leather furniture, and windows on all sides.

Power exited the elevator first and motioned for Ryan to follow. Looking around, Ryan noticed that the "office" took up almost the entire floor of the skyscraper – it was some kind of gigantic loft that offered a magnificent panoramic view of the entire city of Seattle, stretching between Lake Washington and Puget Sound, as well as the mountain ranges extending in every direction along the horizon.

Only their corner of the floor was lit; the rest was shrouded in twilight. Ryan could make out the outlines of various objects. He thought he could see pieces of furniture with massive paintings above them. And was that the silhouette of a sports car?

"Forgive me, Mr. Creed, if I offended you with my question," Power explained. "It was not my intention." He sat down at a large desk.

Ryan sat down across from him in a chair that looked austere but was unexpectedly luxurious. "So what exactly *is* it that you flew me all this way for, Mr. Power? Some kind of riddle, apparently? Let's see it."

Power picked up a leather folder from his desk. He pulled out a page with a photo and handed it to Ryan. "Does this mean anything to you?"

Ryan looked at the picture. "A gold coin. Face value twenty dollars. Although by now its material value is probably many times that."

Power smiled. "That's right. I estimate the actual value of the gold in it to be just under one thousand seven hundred dollars. In this case, however, we're talking about the *collector's* value – and that's inestimable."

Ryan blinked in surprise. "How so?"

"What you see here is an image of the rarest coin in the world: the 1933 Double Eagle. There's exactly one known example in private hands – and it was auctioned off for nearly ten million dollars to an anonymous bidder almost twenty years ago."

Putting down the paper, Ryan got up.

"If you want to recruit me for a burglary, forget it. Not for all the money in the world."

With a mollifying gesture, Power motioned for Ryan to sit back down. "Not at *all*! There's no need to break any laws to accomplish what I want from you. Everything is perfectly legal. I'm not interested in this coin."

With a frown, Ryan sat down. "If you're not interested, why are you showing it to me?"

"I'm not interested in *this* coin – the one that was auctioned off. I'm interested in other, previously *undiscovered* specimens."

"I think you need to start being a little more specific."

"Certainly. What do you associate with the year 1933, Mr. Creed?"

Ryan pondered. "Hitler's rise to power, the premiere of *King Kong*, the end of Prohibition, Franklin Delano Roosevelt becoming president."

"Very good!" Power interrupted him. "FDR took office in the midst of the Great Depression – with the promise of the *New Deal*, a fundamental reform of the economic and social system. And one of his first acts was... what?"

Power gave Ryan a challenging look, like a teacher waiting for an answer from his favorite student.

"I'm not in the mood for a quiz right now, Mr. Power. Say what you have to say or forget it."

Power shook his head. "I had assumed you were better versed in history. Well, one of Roosevelt's first acts was to pass legislation severely restricting private ownership of gold. He also abolished gold coins as a currency. Coincidentally, there was a series of twenty-dollar gold coins minted around the same time. By the time they were produced, they were no longer valid, yet now there were *tons* of them."

Ryan nodded slowly. "So although these coins did exist, they had lost their purpose and were never put into circulation, and don't exist anymore. Except for this one specimen, which is now in the hands of a collector. Have I got a basic grasp *on* the situation?"

"Very close," Power said, once again adopting a professorial tone. "Almost all of the Double Eagles minted in 1933 were melted down. But twenty of them found their way into circulation in some unknown fashion. Nineteen were confiscated by the U.S. government over time. A single coin was finally permitted to remain in private ownership. This is the one that was auctioned off for millions at the time."

"And if it's not *this* one you're after, then I guess you think there's another one out there somewhere?" concluded Ryan.

"Not one, Mr. Creed. Thirty. I'm sure there are thirty 1933 Double Eagles stashed away somewhere. And the puzzle I've given you is the first step in finding them."

Continue reading on page 104.

"*Company scrip*," Ryan repeated when Sarah had finished reading the email reply. "*Company money.* Meaning what the company paid out to the miners one day, they took back the next when people bought their groceries. Nice concept for maximizing profits."

Sarah had found the location of the former Kern & Miller mine on a map on the Internet. "I don't know," she said. "Considering the location, the workers were probably glad to have a store nearby."

Ryan looked at Sarah's phone. "I don't know the area that well, but the mine seems to be in the boondocks. Is that right?"

"Basically. It's one of the most remote corners of the mountains. There's not even a decent road to get up there."

"How did they supply the mine in the old days?"

Sarah shrugged. "No idea. Not with cars or wagons, anyway."

"This is going to be fun." Ryan pointed to Sarah's vest. "You got any mountaineering gear in there?"

Sarah grinned. "No, and we won't need it. We have a much better way to get to the mine. I'll keep it a surprise for you!"

Sarah packed the last of her stuff while Ryan stepped outside to enjoy the morning sun. But as soon as he was out the door, he stopped in alarm.

There was a white SUV parked on the side of the road. Ryan's heart skipped a beat. On closer inspection, he clearly recognized a scratch on the right front fender – the exact same spot where their pursuer had struck the bollard while turning yesterday!

Ryan tried to look relaxed. He strolled to the front desk area and pretended to browse the rack of pamphlets for tourist attractions. Through the lobby window he could see the car, but not its interior. He took a flyer for Mount *St.* Helens and started casually walking back to the room, making a show of reading it as if he'd found an exciting activity for the day. When he arrived, his demeanor changed the moment he closed the door behind him.

"We have to get out of here!" He yelled to Sarah agitatedly. "*Now!* Those guys from yesterday are parked outside!"

Sarah cursed. "Are you sure? This town is absolutely overrun with SUVs."

"Hell *yeah*, I'm sure. It's the same SUV that ambushed us last night! They're after the notebook!"

"Damn, how did they *find* us here?"

"No clue! But we should do our damnedest to stay away from them." He pointed to the window. "Let's go out the back!"

They quickly grabbed their things – after all, they didn't have much luggage – and climbed out the window onto a flower bed at the back of the motel.

"We'll have to leave my car," Sarah said. "They'll be watching for that too."

Sneaking under the cover of bushes and trees, they made their way to the nearest major road, where Sarah hailed a cab.

A few minutes later, they were sitting in the back of a slightly aged taxicab with electronic music blasting from the stereo.

As they put more distance between themselves and the motel, they kept checking behind them, but the white SUV was nowhere to be seen.

"It *can't* just be luck that they found us!" Ryan had moved his mouth right up to Sarah's ear, speaking so softly that the driver couldn't possibly hear him over the blaring music.

"I don't know," Sarah replied in a hushed voice. "Maybe they sent a whole fleet of cars to look for us."

"And put the *one* car we saw yesterday *right* in front of us? I don't think so."

"That could just be a damn coincidence. It happens." She pointed behind her. "Anyway, we've ditched them. And this time they don't stand a chance of catching up with us."

"You said that last time. How can you be so sure this time?"

Sarah smiled. "Like I said, I'll keep it a surprise."

Half an hour later, the driver dropped them off in the parking lot of a small airfield just outside of town. There was a sign in the driveway: *Tackett Helicopter Services.*

So this was what Sarah meant when she said she had a better way to get up into the mountains.

The sky was clear and the airport wasn't very busy. Not yet, Ryan guessed, since it was early in the morning. Sarah nodded to a uniformed airport employee in his mid-fifties. They obviously knew each other.

"Morning, Jack! Is the chopper out?"

Jack was not a man of many words. He mumbled something that could probably be interpreted as a "yep" and cocked his head toward the apron, where a helicopter was waiting outside a hangar.

"I still don't understand how they knew we were at the motel," Ryan mused as they walked to the plane.

Sarah groaned. "Are you going to start *that* crap again?"

"Could they have put a tracking device on your car?"

"It's possible," Sarah replied curtly, quickening her pace.

"*It's possible*?" Ryan repeated incredulously. "Doesn't that even bother you?"

"Not at the moment. They found us and we lost them. That's the end of it."

Ryan didn't let up. "What if they find us *again*?"

Abruptly, Sarah stopped walking and turned to Ryan. "How are they going to do that? Yeah, maybe they had a tracker on my car. *Congratulations*, it's still at the motel. And this helicopter definitely doesn't have a tracking device – Jack checked it thoroughly just this morning. Even if he doesn't talk any more than he has to, if he had noticed something, he would tell me."

Ryan shrugged and didn't respond. Sarah's reaction reminded him of her sudden brusqueness last night when she thought he was going to ask her something private. Was there something she didn't want to tell him? Or was she just offended because she felt he was questioning her competence?

They continued to the helicopter. "Get in," Sarah instructed Ryan. "I'll do the walk-around. And *please* don't touch anything inside."

"Wait: *you're* flying?" Ryan said haltingly.

Sarah looked at him with disdain. "I come from an aviation family. My dad was an engineer for a major airline. I was practically *born* with a pilot's license."

As Sarah began to inspect the outside of the machine, Ryan climbed aboard.

It wasn't the first time he'd been in a helicopter. This one was quite small; there was less room in the cabin than in Ryan's car, but it looked like four people could just about squeeze in.

He watched Sarah, who was still diligently checking that everything was in order. The thing about her dad had been the first piece of private information she had shared with him. But was it the truth? Sarah was still a bit of a riddle to him. And some riddles came with misleading clues.

He wondered how she came to work for Will Power. And if she had a special position there, if she was something like his right hand, or if there were more assistants like her.

This whole mission was so well prepared and equipped that it didn't seem like Power and Sarah were doing it for the first time. There was experience behind it all. It was quite possible that Power really wasn't involved in any illegal business – but Ryan was pretty sure that he didn't spend his days counting the income from his properties, either.

A few minutes later, Sarah came on board and handed him a pair of headphones. "Put these on. Once the rotor starts, we won't be able to hear each other."

She showed him the button to press if he wanted to talk to her and asked him to be quiet until they had completed takeoff. She needed to concentrate.

Although that was probably true, Ryan had the distinct feeling that Sarah was quite happy not to have to talk to him right now. He just couldn't figure out why.

"Sea-Tac Traffic, Helicopter 2191K taking off at the hangars for a northeast departure, initial climb 1000 feet, Sea-Tac Traffic."

Ryan wasn't familiar with aviation communications, but Sarah's announcements were so routine they had to come from years of experience. The helicopter rose slowly into the air. The thick headphones muted the engine noise to a low hum, and the beauty of Puget Sound stretched out before Ryan's eyes. He saw the waves lapping against the shore, the skyscrapers of downtown Seattle with the Space Needle standing out as a landmark, and beyond that, the slopes and peaks of the Cascade Range rising to Seattle's east.

"The mine is over there," Sarah said after a few minutes, pointing to the mountains. "But we'll have to take a detour so we don't get in the way of the big planes. I hope that's not a problem."

"No, not at all," Ryan replied. "I'm just going to enjoy the view for now."

And it was truly spectacular. The area around Seattle was considered one of the most scenic in the United States. People who came here didn't have to choose between the mountains or the ocean; they had both. Wilderness *and* big city. He was a little envious that Sarah got to live here.

"You're lucky it's so clear. There are plenty of days when you can't even see the mountains."

Sarah's friendliness seemed like an attempt to make up for her earlier taciturnity. Ryan was happy to accept the offer and adopted a similarly conciliatory attitude.

"I didn't expect this when you picked me up yesterday morning, but I'm starting to enjoy this whole thing. Despite those weird guys earlier."

Yesterday morning. It really was barely twenty-four hours since he had been uprooted from his daily routine.

Sarah smiled. "Did we bring out the adventurer in you?"

"No, but this is so... how can I put it? *Tangible.* No numbers in a computer, no pencil and eraser – we're really experiencing the world! I guess I should be thanking you for this."

Sarah suddenly became serious. "Don't thank us too soon."

"Why's that? You told me Power was a man of his word. We'll either find the coins, or we'll find that they're no longer there. Either way, I'll have done my job."

Sarah hesitated for a moment, as if she wanted to say something, but then she just nodded. "Yeah, you're probably right."

But she didn't sound very convinced.

Maybe it had been naive to trust this Power guy so much, Ryan thought. Sarah had known him longer than he had, and she seemed skeptical. But what was the worst that could happen? Power cheating him out of his reward? Well, that would be annoying, but hardly the end of the world.

No matter how Ryan looked at it, it still didn't seem like he had much to lose. Then again, he knew from painful experience what it meant to trust the wrong people.

Continue reading on page 059.

"1, 2, 5 – and open!" Ryan had carefully set the combination, and sure enough, with a clatter, the antique locking mechanism began to move. He pulled on the metal bar and the safe door opened.

The drawer behind it wasn't very big – it wouldn't even hold a shoebox – but it didn't need to be big, because it contained something very small: a round, shiny coin, a little bigger than a quarter!

"Is that a Double Eagle?" Ryan exclaimed.

"Nope," Sarah replied. "They're bigger and thicker. I'm not even sure it's money."

She carefully reached into the safe and picked up the coin. As the flashlight's beam fell on it, Ryan realized that Sarah was right: although it was a round, embossed piece of metal, it didn't seem to match any currency he knew. A geometric shape was imprinted in the center, and letters were engraved in a circle around it on the front and back. But the coin was too worn to read the inscription.

If it wasn't money, what else could it be? Maybe a token from a casino or an old vending machine? And if it was, how would they find that?

"Have you seen anything like a slot machine down here?" he asked Sarah.

She shook her head. "But other than this hidden room, nothing else looks like it did in Dash's day."

That made sense. If there was anything left to find, it would be in the room behind the wall.

Ryan carefully crawled through the hole in the wall and looked around.

All the objects and furniture had been nailed down securely and had survived decades without shifting or falling over. And there was not the slightest hint of another secret hidden here.

"I give up," he sighed finally. "Whatever this thing is supposed to tell us, it doesn't seem to have anything to do with this room."

"OK." Sarah yawned. "I think it's time to wrap things up for today and approach this with a fresh perspective tomorrow."

As was often the case, the way back was faster than getting there. They knew where to go now, and they knew the tunnels to take. On the way, Ryan looked around for more of Reginald Dash's monograms, but he found nothing.

It was already dark when they returned to the small square outside. Sarah carefully locked the door with her lockpick, then they made their way to the car.

When Sarah opened the car door, the interior lights illuminated a couple of shopping bags in the back seat.

"Those are for you," she informed Ryan. "So you'll have something fresh to wear tomorrow."

"You're telling me that you and Mr. Power figured out my clothes size?"

Sarah grinned. "You don't have to be a great spy for *that*. A size medium shirt, anyone can see that. And your jeans have the size printed right above the back pockets."

"You've been looking at my butt?" Ryan countered in amusement.

"Strictly professional," Sarah countered. "So don't get too excited."

They got into the car and Ryan had to admit to himself yet again that he was having fun. More fun than he'd ever had in his job as a lecturer. And Sarah was better company than most of his colleagues back home.

The car began to move. Ryan looked back at the decrepit plot of land they had just been exploring beneath. From out here, there was nothing to suggest the existence of a hidden world down there.

He was about to turn back around when a movement caught his attention. Just behind them, a car started up and pulled out of the parking lot. For a moment, before the headlights blinded him, Ryan caught a glimpse of the vehicle – and it looked very familiar. It was undoubtedly the white SUV he had seen when they were entering the store earlier!

"I think we're being followed," Ryan whispered to Sarah – and immediately wondered why he was speaking so quietly. It wasn't like anyone in the other car could hear them!

"Are you sure?"

"Pretty sure. The car was circling the area earlier, it was parked nearby, pulled out just after we did, and now it's keeping a safe distance from us."

"It could be a coincidence," Sarah said. "We're heading downtown. It's a busy area."

"Signal right," Ryan replied.

"Why? We have to go straight."

"I didn't say actually *turn* right, I just said signal right. Signal, get in the right lane, and then go straight. I want to see what the other car does."

"Right," Sarah said. "I should've thought of that."

Sarah moved into the turn lane and soon the white car pulled up behind them and started to signal. Catching a glimpse of it in her rearview mirror, Sarah grumbled under her breath. She stayed in the right lane until just before the light, then accelerated at the last moment, swerving to the left and changing lanes.

An indignant honk could be heard behind them, but Sarah ignored it. "Is the car still following us?" she asked Ryan.

His eyes scanned the flow of traffic for the white SUV – and found it. It, too, was edging back into their lane, scraping against a concrete bollard on its way.

"It's still there," he confirmed.

Sarah cursed. "This is *all* we need." She accelerated a little but kept up with the flow of traffic.

Ryan looked at Dash's notebook in his hands. "You want to bet that's what they're looking for?"

"What *else* would they be looking for? I doubt they want your new outfit."

"But who *are* they? And how do they know?"

"You said it yourself earlier," Sarah replied, not taking her eyes off the road. "The book is worth a couple hundred million. When that kind of money is involved, word gets around eventually, no matter what you do."

She glanced briefly in the rearview mirror and then at Ryan. "I promised you earlier that we wouldn't do anything illegal, except for a little trespassing."

"Yeah, and?" Ryan didn't understand what she was getting at.

"I lied. We aren't sticking to the speed limit, either."

Before Ryan could say anything, she slammed her foot down on the accelerator. The car sped so fast that Ryan was pinned to his seat. His right hand gripped the passenger door as Sarah zigzagged around the other drivers.

Amid screeching tires and indignant honking, Sarah's car made its way through the evening traffic. Ryan turned to see the white SUV trying to keep up but losing ground.

"Watch out, hold on!" Sarah yelled, spinning the car abruptly around a street corner. The wheels skidded sideways across the asphalt, threatening to lose traction, but Sarah regained control of the vehicle with a well-timed jab of the accelerator.

"This isn't the first time you've done this, is it?" Ryan said as they sped through a lane barely wider than their car.

"Like I said, when you work for Will, it's good to have some special skills."

And with those words, Sarah yanked the wheel around again, sending the car rocketing out onto a busy main road. Ryan had no idea how Sarah managed to avoid an accident. Behind them, horns honked wildly as other cars braked or swerved to avoid them, but after a few seconds, she had managed to merge into the flow of traffic.

Ryan scanned the roads around them, then breathed a sigh of relief. "I think you managed to lose them."

Continue reading on page 097.

Clues and Answers

There are three clues for each riddle. The page number for each riddle is written at the end of each row. If you get stuck, simply look for the page number of the riddle you need help with.

Then look for the first red shape at the left of that row and place the red plastic film (from the back cover flap) on top. You will now see a clue that will help you move forward. If the first clue doesn't do the trick, take a look at the middle shape for more hints. The third has the answer.

Be sure to check off each box, so you know how many clues you've used. (If a hint only tells you things you already figured out, you don't have to check the box.)

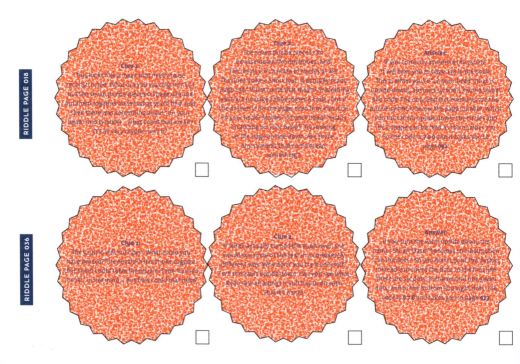

RIDDLE PAGE 018

Clue 1:
This looks like a maze that needs to be reconstructed. What are you waiting for? Cut out the seven puzzle pieces on page 029 and put them together to see what you'll find. And then there was something about "on your head" and symbols ... what could that mean? It's all very cryptic, isn't it?

☐

Clue 2:
The seven puzzle pieces can be assembled like dominoes. And the result isn't a maze of routes at all! The lines make a short text. It actually reads "page 138." What could that mean? Something abstract on page 138 becomes a code , but if the answer is on the page, then how can it be on your head? Maybe "on your head" means "standing on your head"! Try looking at the page upside down. Are there any symbols that could mean something?

☐

Answer:
If you correctly assemble the puzzle, it will take you to page 138 in the book. There, when you're "on your head" (that is, upside down), abstract symbols should reveal the code. The only abstract elements are the puzzle symbols below the page number. When you turn them upside down, the circles and the L shape can be read as the number 700. So the code is **7 0 0** and it takes you to page **092**.

☐

RIDDLE PAGE 036

Clue 1:
The vault is still not open. What could you have missed? The puzzle instructions suggest that Sarah could solve the puzzle if she "turned it over" in her mind ... but how could that help?

☐

Clue 2:
If Sarah actually turned the vault over, she would see some of the text in a completely different way. Why don't you try it yourself? Turn the vault upside down. Can you see what Ryan saw all along? It still has to do with Stuart's name.

☐

Answer:
If you turn the vault upside down, the name "Stuart Dash" becomes the instruction "use the dots." So you don't count the dashes; instead you count the dots. In the first line there are six dots, in the second line seven dots, and in the bottom line eight dots. The code is **6 7 8** and takes you to page **023**.

☐

1 8 5

RIDDLE PAGE 049

RIDDLE PAGE 069

RIDDLE PAGE 075

RIDDLE PAGE 080

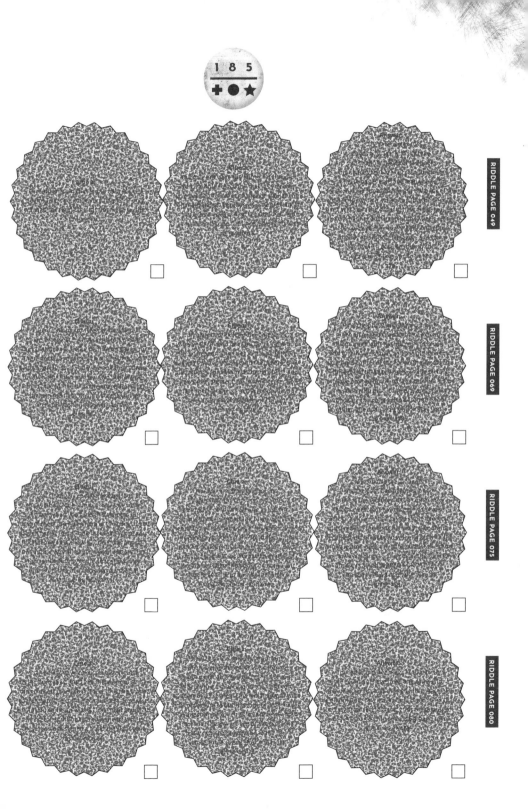

RIDDLE PAGE 106

Clue 1

[illegible]

Clue 2

[illegible]

Answer

[illegible]

RIDDLE PAGE 113

Clue 1

[illegible]

Clue 2

[illegible]

Answer

[illegible]

RIDDLE PAGE 117

Clue 1

[illegible]

Clue 2

[illegible]

Answer

[illegible]

RIDDLE PAGE 125

Clue 1

[illegible]

Clue 2

[illegible]

Answer

[illegible]

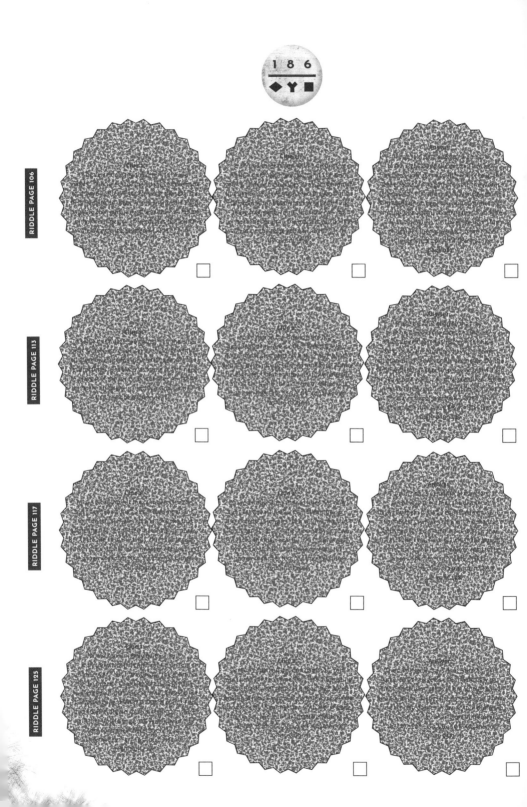

RIDDLE PAGE 139

Clue 1:

The notebook entry looks helpful. You can also find signposts A, B, and C on page 135. The pencils indicate that you should trace certain sections of the routes. What remains to be figured out is how to navigate through the maze. What if the path leads to the edge of the map or into a tunnel?

Clue 2:

The entry reveals that on route A, you should trace all the sections with stone piles. On route B, do the same with the coal piles, and on route C use the wooden planks. Where the path leads to the edge of the map, continue at the same point on the other side. And if it leads into a tunnel, it must also lead out of a tunnel. The wagons will be helpful here. Eventually, you should see the light!

Answer:

Follow the routes from start to finish, tracing the sections with stones (A), coal (B), or wooden planks (C). If the path leads into a tunnel, continue at the tunnel with an identical wagon. If you have chosen the correct routes and followed them to the finish, the sections you have traced, when held up to a light and sorted by the color of the decoding strips, give the code **2 6 8**, which takes you to page **037**.

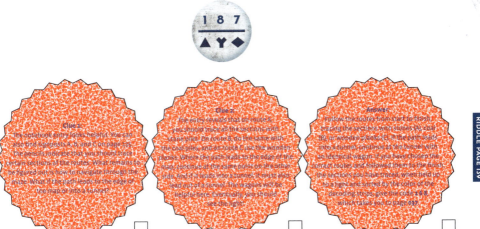

How many clues did you use?

Count how many boxes you checked in the "Clues and Answers" section.

0 You are a total riddle genius. Incredible performance! Congratulations!

1–3 You've done remarkably well and should be proud of yourself!

4–8 Wow! You're really good at this! A very respectable score!

9–13 Nice job, you got through with a hint here and there.

14–18 Not bad at all. There's every reason to feel good about yourself.

19–22 OK, not the best result – but not the worst either.

23–27 We're sure you can do better, and with less help than you may think.

28–30 Don't be disappointed. There's always next time.

Challenge yourself to other puzzle novels in the EXIT: THE BOOK series!

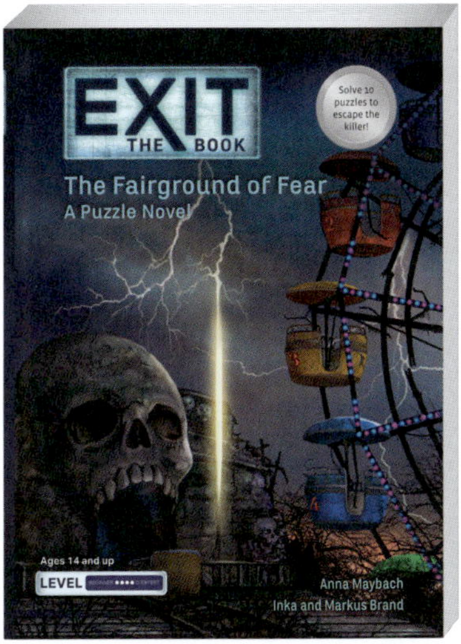

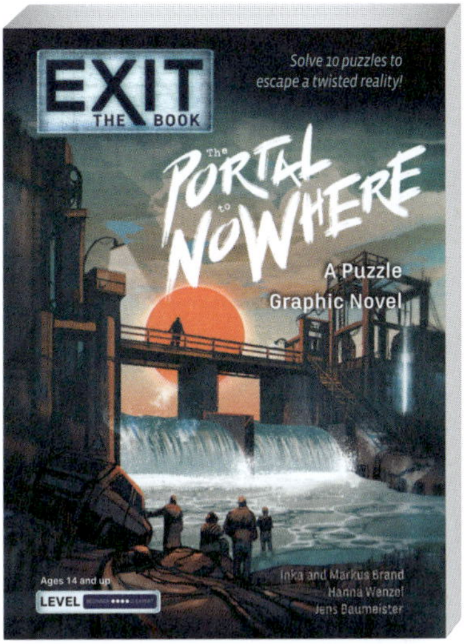

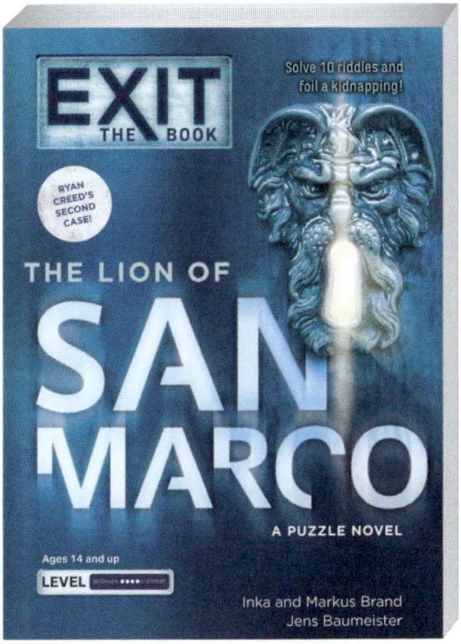

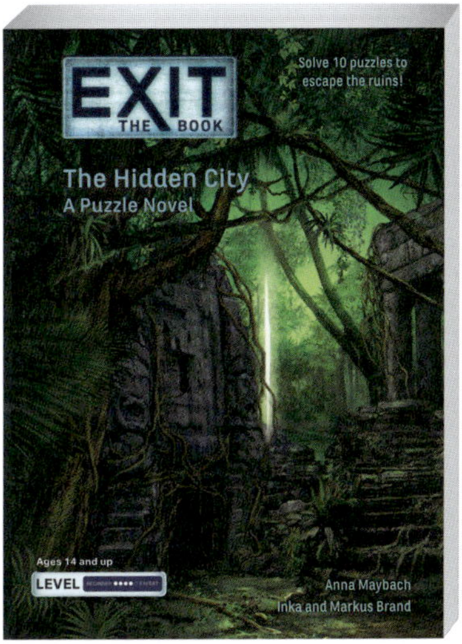

Decoding Made Easy

To solve each riddle, you must find the three-digit code which will take you to the page number on which the story continues.

How to use the decoding strips:

1. Enter the three numbers from the solved riddle by moving the colored strips on the front decoding flap so that the digits line up with the arrow.
2. Now turn the decoding flap over. The arrow will point to a new three-digit number with symbols above.
3. This three-digit code is the page number on which the story continues.
4. Check to see if the symbol above each digit on the decoding strip matches the symbols below the page number in the book.
5. If the symbols on the book page match the symbols on your decoding strips, you have solved the riddle and can continue with the story.
6. If the symbols do not match, you have not solved the riddle. Please try again.

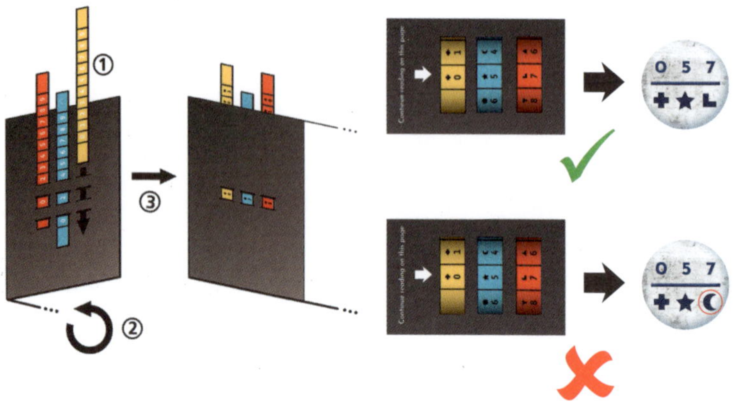

	0	1	2	3	4	5	6	7	8	9	
	0	1	2	3	4	5	6	7	8	9	
	0	1	2	3	4	5	6	7	8	9	

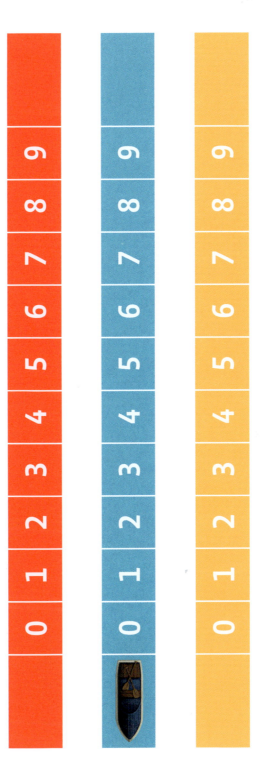

Cut out decoding strips here

✚	◆	⬢	●	★	☾	▲	L	Y	■
0	1	0	1	0	1	0	1	0	1

✚	◆	⬢	●	★	☾	▲	L	Y	■
9	8	7	6	5	4	3	2	1	0

■	Y	L	▲	☾	★	●	⬢	◆	✚
9	8	7	6	5	4	3	2	1	0

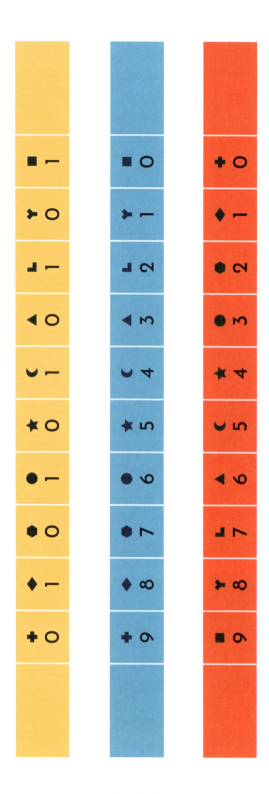

Cut out decoding strips here